D0249236

"I'm not a snob."

"Really?" He took the decoration, their fingers brushing.

Her skin tingled even after he'd pulled away. "You don't have to sound so surprised."

Desire danced in the air, an electricity between them as he moved closer to her. "Would it soften the sting to your ego if I told you how hot you look no matter what you're wearing?"

She closed her hand into a fist, trying to will away the lingering sensation of that simple touch. "And what about those three bridal prospects of yours, one of whom will give you babies to make Christmas memories with?"

He canted back, nodding tightly. "You're right. It's totally inappropriate of me. I mean it when I say I want to be a family man, and all that entails."

"The epitome of a Texas Cattleman's Club fella."

"Yes, exactly that." His gaze held hers, setting her skin on fire with just the stroke of his eyes on her face.

Even knowing it was unwise and there were so many reasons they were wrong for each other, she still felt herself sway toward him. Just one kiss.

* * *

Hot Holiday Rancher is part of the Texas Cattleman's Club: Houston series.

Dear Reader,

I so enjoy the Christmas season and celebrating with family—the one we were born into and the one we create for ourselves. Yes, the Texas Cattleman's Club novels are full of dynamic, loving and sometimes feuding families. But I especially enjoy how this fan-favorite ongoing series also showcases friendships that grow into a beautiful extended family network. So that made this particular TCC novel a treat for me to write in their world by featuring the opening of a whole new chapter in Houston.

Whether you're a longtime reader of the Texas Cattleman Club stories or are new to the TCC community, thank you for picking up *Hot Holiday Rancher*!

Merry Christmas!

Cathy Mann

www.CatherineMann.com

CATHERINE MANN

—

HOT HOLIDAY RANCHER

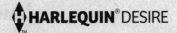

HARLEQUIN® DESIRE

Recycling programs
for this product may
not exist in your area.

ISBN-13: 978-1-335-60398-2

Hot Holiday Rancher

Copyright © 2019 by Harlequin Books S.A.

This edition published by arrangement with Harlequin Books S.A.

For questions and comments about the quality of this book,
please contact us at CustomerService@Harlequin.com.

Printed in U.S.A.

Books by Catherine Mann

Harlequin Desire

Alaskan Oil Barons

Texas Cattleman's Club: Houston

To my children, the best gift all year round!

One

Esme Perry had basked in the sun on a private beach in the South of France. She'd surfed with the best of them in California, Hawaii and Australia. But not even the threat of heatstroke or sharks had concerned her as much as the rush of water rolling down the country Texas back road toward her low-slung Porsche.

Rain sheeting against her windshield, Esme shifted into Reverse, willing her pulse to slow. *Be calm. Take deep breaths.* A quick three-point turn should have her ready to race out of harm's way. It would be a tight maneuver since the road was narrow, bracketed by a ditch on one side and sycamore trees on the other. It was tough enough to make such a maneuver during the daytime, but after dark? In the middle of a storm?

Not that she had a choice but to move. Flash floods were dangerous, especially in the country.

But her V-8 engine could outrace just about anything. Perhaps the Porsche wasn't the best choice for dirt roads, but she'd been excited about her early Christmas gift to herself.

Two points into Esme's three-point turn, the wave of rainwater slammed into the side of her vehicle. Her stomach clenched. She struggled to control the steering wheel as her car slid along the mud-slicked road. The Porsche's back end fishtailed. Her foot slipped off the clutch, her spiky heel wedging under the brake. The heel snapped. But she didn't have time to mourn the demise of her favorite leopard-print pumps. The Porsche lurched, then spun out, whipping the wheel from her clenched grip.

Her heart rose into her throat with panic as she battled what felt like g-forces slamming her against the door. Worse yet, she couldn't see due to vertigo and the rush of water over her candy apple–red hood. Was she close to the side of the road? How deep was the ditch? Where were the trees?

And, oh God, were those headlights or lampposts?

She braced. Struggled not to close her eyes. And prayed.

The spinning stopped, her car halting with a jolt. But not a crash. She exhaled a shaky breath, her ears ringing so loudly it almost drowned out the rain pounding the roof and a Christmas carol flowing from the speaker.

"Silent Night"?

Hardly.

But she was all right, in one piece, as was her car. With luck, she could still reach her destination before bedtime. She would have arrived earlier, but an accident on the interstate from Houston to Royal had delayed her arrival. At least she was close enough to her destination to walk. According to her GPS, the front gate to Jesse Stevens's ranch should be less than a mile away.

She pressed the clutch, threw the car into Neutral and pressed the ignition.

The engine turned over. Then spluttered out.

She tried again and...

Nothing. Not even a catch.

She'd bought the stick-shift model, a purist when it came to her sports cars. She liked the control of a manual transmission, a talent she'd learned when teaching herself to drive on one of her father's older trucks on their Houston ranch. She'd been determined to perfect the skill, to win his approval.

Not much had changed on that front, since she

was here to please her dad, to bolster his image with the charter branch of the Texas Cattleman's Club here in Royal, in hopes that he could be president of the new Houston branch.

Her PR plan would start with a surprise visit to Royal's own Jesse Stevens, an influential player at the TCC. If she could ever get there.

She bit back a curse, weighing her options. The odds of a tow truck showing up out here in this weather were slim. Should she wait to see if the car started and risk getting hit by another wave? Or start walking? In her broken shoes. In the rain. And mud. Sighing in resignation, she angled to get her umbrella.

Bracing, she opened the door, and rain sheeted inside. She wedged her umbrella through the opening, although it was fast becoming a moot point. Even her Prada trench was losing the fight against the deluge. Frigid water lapped around her ankles, soaking the hem of her slacks as she leaned into the wind, shivering. Still, she was determined to forge ahead, one step at a time.

She couldn't bear the thought of telling her father she needed to postpone the promotion trip. He'd put his trust in her, and even knowing a thirty-four-year-old woman shouldn't care this much what her father thought, she couldn't deny she was still trying to win his approval, to be something other than the often-forgotten middle child.

In college, she'd found her niche with an aptitude for public relations. It was her chance to shine. When her father had taken note of her success after graduation, he'd hired her as PR executive for the family business, Perry Holdings.

And if ever Sterling Perry had needed a promotional face-lift, it was now, when the new Houston Texas Cattleman's Club was cranking up. Fledgling organizations hated nothing more than a scandal.

And her father's good name had taken quite a few blows, first with an arrest on charges of orchestrating a Ponzi scheme that nearly caused a collapse of one of his investment funds.

No sooner had her father gotten out from under the weight of the fraud rumors than he was under suspicion for the murder of a Perry Holdings assistant. And, as if her father wasn't already stressed enough, just last week a Currin Oil executive named Willem Inwood had been arrested under suspicion of being behind the Ponzi scheme. He wasn't talking yet, but already people were coming forward saying he was the one who'd started those nasty rumors.

Now, even though his innocence had been proven on the murder charge and Ponzi issue, he still needed a serious image makeover if he expected to win the club's leadership spot.

And she intended to give him that fresh start, with some help from Jesse Stevens. Wrestling her bedraggled umbrella, she trudged ahead another couple of steps.

Were those lights flickering ahead? Hope and wariness jockeyed inside her. She was so very cold and soggy. But this also wasn't Houston, with her high-rise condo secured by round-the-clock guards.

She pulled one hand from the umbrella and reached inside her coat to her cross-body bag, fumbling for her can of Mace.

The lights drew closer, grew stronger, until the glow focused into two beams. High off the ground. A truck. The driver's-side door swung wide and a large, looming figure jumped out, ducking into the rain while holding his Stetson in place.

She gripped her Mace harder. She'd taken self-defense classes in college, but she was seriously off-balance with one broken heel and the other spiked into the mud.

"Ma'am, what are you doing out here tonight? Are you waiting for a tow truck?"

That voice. It couldn't be… But her ears told her it was. After all, she'd spent countless hours watching videos of Jesse Stevens giving interviews, memorized them, in fact, to decide the best tactic for approaching him. She tilted her head to catch sight of his face below the brim to confirm.

And she gasped.

No picture could do him justice. Even with the Stetson covering his blond hair, he bore the look of a cowboy Viking. An image she found difficult to let go of once it came to life in her mind.

Spluttering on a mouthful of rain, she tucked her Mace can back into her purse, no longer needing protection.

She should have suspected the truck could belong to Jesse Stevens. She was near his ranch, after all. But still, weren't the odds higher it would be one of his employees rather than him at this hour, in the rain?

Yet there was no doubting who this man was, even in the dark with just his headlights slicing through the night. She'd done her research on the man and his spread well before this excursion to meet him, persuade him.

But she wasn't ready to let him know who she was. Not just yet. She swallowed hard. "My car won't start, and the cell reception is garbage out here in the middle of nowhere."

"Speaking as the landlord of the Middle of Nowhere, I've never had any trouble with mine." Rain dripped from the brim of his hat as he towered over her. "You should check with your provider."

Was that irony or irritation coating his words?

Not good if she'd already made him angry. This would be over before it started.

She longed for higher heels to make her taller, closer to his eye level. "I'll be sure to look into my provider as soon as I find dry clothes. If you could just help me call for a tow, I'll get my suitcase so I can change. I'm freezing to death."

It was cold for Texas, even in December.

"Your car's not going anywhere tonight, ma'am. And there's no way either of us should risk walking back over to your vehicle to retrieve your luggage. The ground could give way at any time."

Her foot slipped. She looked quickly at him. "It's just my broken shoe."

Then her other foot shot out from under her. She lurched to the side, her umbrella whipping away in the wind. Her arms pinwheeled as she lost her balance, tumbling toward the rushing swell of water alongside the dirt road.

Strong hands clasped her waist and stopped her fall. Before she could catch her breath, he'd hauled her against his chest. His warm breath fanned her cheek.

"Are you all right?"

Other than goose bumps that had nothing to do with the cold because she was in the arms of a Viking cowboy? "I'm fine." Her words came out husky. "Thank you."

"What are you doing out here this time of night in such crummy weather?" Thunder rolled in the distance.

She braced her palms on his impossibly broad shoulders and looked straight into Jesse Stevens's emerald green eyes. "I'm looking for you."

* * *

Jesse Stevens held the drenched woman against him, her willowy body enticing even through her soaked raincoat and his hastily-tossed-on jacket. He'd been making a last check of the horses, concerned about the thunder spooking them, when he'd seen the car lights. He'd been surprised, not expecting anyone until tomorrow. Not that he was complaining.

The matchmaker he'd hired had outdone herself in sending this candidate.

He wondered which of the three contenders this was—the single mom, the veterinarian or the Miss Texas pageant runner-up. This woman certainly could be the latter, and that might explain the high heels and flashy car choice. The height seemed to be right, based on the stats in her profile. Although it was difficult to tell much in the dark. He was definitely curious to learn more about the husky-voiced siren. All the more reason to resist the temptation to hold on for an extra second or two.

Stepping back, he still cupped her elbow. Just to make sure she didn't lose her balance, of course. "Are you okay? You weren't hurt when your car spun out, were you?"

She nodded, pulling one foot, then the other, out of the mud. "I'm fine, thank you. I truly didn't expect the weather to get this bad."

Given her slick trench and Porsche, she had more

of a city-girl vibe that he had doubts would hold up out here. But the matchmaker would have told her about him and his rural lifestyle. He'd sure filled out a checklist of his criteria for the kind of woman he was looking for.

"Ma'am, the road is at risk of giving way further. You need to get to safety. My truck can take an alternate path that's not accessible to the public."

"Let's go, then." She started forward, her purse tucked tight to her side, but her foot sank deeper into the mud, stopping her progress. Sighing, she cursed under her breath. Like a sailor, no less.

An unexpected surprise. She had grit to go along with all of that glam. He could still feel the imprint of her against him.

She glanced up at him, her eyelashes spiky wet, her ponytail slick and sleek down the front of her coat. "The heels aren't holding up well out here."

"Then I'll carry you." He wasn't sure where the invitation came from, but now that he'd said it, the idea had taken root. An appealing option, and with each passing second, an increasingly necessary one.

"Whoa, wait." She held up a manicured hand, with two chipped nails and another broken. "That's a bit extreme."

"Ma'am…" He smiled. "The longer we talk, the worse the roads will be. And I don't know about you, but I'm cold even though I have on boots."

Indecision flickered across her face. But then she

shivered and her hand lowered. She nodded quickly, her teeth chattering.

All the invitation he needed.

He scooped her up into his arms, tucking her against him as he made tracks toward his truck. With a squeak of surprise, she looped her arms around his neck, a light scent of something floral and exotic riding the humid air to tempt his nose. Her body fit against him, the curve of her breast pressed to him.

So much for feeling cold. Heat fired through his veins. But he needed to learn more about her. His days of sowing wild oats were in the past. He was ready to settle down, build a family, and he wasn't waiting around for chance to bring him the woman he needed.

He'd contacted a selective, high-priced match-maker to assist him in the search. His days were packed with running his ranch. His only social life involved the occasional event at the Texas Cattle-man's Club and he already knew every one of the members. He wanted a wife, children—heirs. He didn't believe in grand romance or love. But he was a firm advocate of the benefits of a winning part-nership.

Yes, he more than wanted a wife. He *needed* a wife and he was prepared to offer that spouse his full partnership in return. A win-win for them both.

Once he found the right candidate.

Stopping by the passenger side of his dual-cab truck, he set the woman on her feet carefully, ensuring the ground beneath her was safe before he let go. The rain was coming down in buckets.

He opened the door for her, offering a hand as she stepped on the running board. Damn, those dainty shoes of hers were mighty mangled. She hadn't been prepared. The clasp of her cold fingers in his hand reminded him of how badly this stormy evening could have turned out for her.

And it still could if he didn't get his butt in gear and drive back to the house. He braced a hand on the hood as he jogged around to the driver's side. Once behind the wheel, he slammed his door closed against the wall of rain being blown inside.

At least the heater was still blasting, since he'd never turned the vehicle off. He swept aside his Stetson, flinging it to the back seat beside a horse blanket and a thermos.

"I'm so glad you came along," she said, her teeth still chattering. She kicked off her broken shoes and wriggled her toes under the blast of warm air circling at the floorboard.

"And I'm glad I saw you out there." He started to ask her name, but the rain picked up pace on the roof. It could wait. "I hate to think what could have happened to you if those waters swept your car away."

As she'd said right away, she knew who he was.

So he didn't have to worry about reassuring her she was safe to come with him.

"You were right to question the wisdom of my driving into this storm," she conceded. "I was so eager to get here, I just kept thinking I could outpace the weather."

She shook her head, laughing softly. The husky melody of her chuckle filled the truck cab, stroking his senses. That matchmaker sure had a knack.

He cleared his throat. "And the weather still might win if we don't get moving."

Jesse eased the four-wheel-drive vehicle out of Park and accelerated carefully. The tires spun, then caught, the truck surging forward, toward the dim twinkling of Christmas lights strung along the split-rail fence. The storm smudged the glow until it was just a smear of green, red and white.

"I'm sorry to inconvenience you so late," she said. "I certainly intended to arrive earlier." The truck jostled along a rut in the road and she braced a hand against the door.

"You'd have had better luck with a utility vehicle instead of that sports car of yours."

"It would appear so." She squeezed excess water from her ponytail, her wet hair clearly blond now in the glow of the dash.

But he wasn't any closer to identifying which of the matchmaker's candidates she might be.

"I'm Jesse Stevens, as you already seem to know. And you are?"

"Esme Perry. Nice to meet you, Jesse."

He looked over sharply in surprise at her name. She was not one of the three women the matchmaker had provided. Surely he couldn't have forgotten a recommended candidate. Perhaps he'd missed an email from the matchmaker?

Except… Wait… Alarms sounded in the back of his mind. There were plenty of Perrys in Texas. But one branch in particular was heavy-duty on the radar of the Royal branch of the Texas Cattleman's Club. "Perry, as in…"

"Yes, my father is Sterling Perry. We're very excited about the new branch of the Texas Cattleman's Club opening in Houston. My father sent me here to talk to you. To do a little recon," she said with a sassy smile.

Disappointment churned. She hadn't been sent by the matchmaker. He focused on the path ahead, a back road on higher ground to his home.

"A spy in our midst," he said dryly. Granted, one helluva sexy Mata Hari.

"Not anything so nefarious." She tugged at the belt of her trench coat. "I'm just here to see how you run things at the Royal branch."

"Or to curry favor for your dad."

She straightened in the seat, clearly bristling at the criticism of her father. But it wasn't any secret that Sterling Perry had a sketchy past and a quest for power.

A quest that was currently playing out in a battle with Ryder Currin as they vied for control of the new Houston branch, to be opened in a historic building site, a former luxury boutique hotel. Ryder Currin was a self-made man. Whereas Esme's family was led by the old-money, charming, larger-than-life patriarch Sterling Perry, who continued to grow the Perry fortune in banking, real estate and property development.

Jesse's impression of the man? All show but little substance.

Was this woman like her dad? It seemed so, judging by her car and her clothes and her defense of her father.

He pulled up to his ranch home. More lights glimmered in the trees lining the driveway, and a wreath glowed on the front door of his white two-story house. A sprawling place he'd had built with hopes of one day having a family of his own. His parents were dead. He only had one sister, and while he loved her, she had her own life.

Now he was ready to build a future for himself.

Keeping his eyes off the woman beside him, he steered off the path and onto the driveway, circling around back. More twinkling lights marked the way. He'd arranged for decorations outdoors to make his place more welcoming, but hadn't gotten around to the indoors. His life definitely needed a woman's touch.

He activated the garage door opener, steered into the six-bay garage, and turned off the truck as the automatic door closed behind them. "You can stay at my place until morning…or until the weather blows over."

"I appreciate the offer. Clearly, I'm in no position to turn you down." She gestured to her bare feet and soggy clothes.

"Call it club loyalty. It would be irresponsible of me to send you back out into this weather." He draped a hand over the steering wheel and allowed himself an unrestrained look at the bombshell beside him. "But I don't talk about club business in my off-hours, so I won't be discussing your father or the Houston chapter."

"Fair enough. I just have one question, nothing about the Texas Cattleman's Club." She tipped her head to one side, her raincoat parting to reveal the curve of her breasts in the soaked silk shirt. "Who did you think I was?"

Two

Toying with her seat belt and not in any hurry to leave the truck just yet, Esme waited for Jesse's answer, more curious than she would have liked to admit about what mystery woman he was expecting. Even knowing that cowboys weren't her type, she couldn't deny the appeal of those piercing green eyes.

He cocked an eyebrow as he reached for his Stetson. "I certainly didn't think you were one of the infamous Perry family."

She bristled at the censure in his voice. *"Infamous?"* she repeated, the bubble of romance officially burst. She unbuckled her seat belt and reached for the door handle. "That's rather harsh, don't you think?"

"I didn't mean to offend," he said as his boots hit the pristine cement floor of his six-car garage with a solid thud. "Your father was investigated on fraud charges and the murder of a Perry Holdings assistant not too long ago."

Vincent Hamm had gone missing, the assistant presumed to have quit and moved to the British Virgin Islands to spend his life surfing, based on a text he'd sent his boss. But then his body had been discovered with a bullet wound to the chest, his skull bashed, making identification difficult. But DNA tests had confirmed the man's identity.

Esme slammed the door, the sound reverberating in the dimly lit space. Her damp and muddy feet slipped ever so slightly as she charged forward alongside a speedboat, her toes still so icy cold, her mangled shoes dangling from her hand. An SUV, a motorcycle and a pair of four-wheelers filled the rest of the space. The man sure liked his toys.

Or maybe his family did?

She glanced at his left hand as he tapped the security code at the door leading into the house. No ring. But then, there was still the mystery woman.

Esme pulled her focus back to her reason for being here. To clean up her father's image among the Texas Cattleman's Club members here in Royal.

"My father was cleared of fraud *and* the murder

of Vincent Hamm." All hell had broken loose when the body was found at the site of the new Texas Cattleman's Club, where her father's construction company was doing the renovations. The murderer still hadn't been found. "As I recall, you were under suspicion, too, after leaving an angry message on Hamm's voice mail."

"Valid point." He waved her inside with a broad hand, his square jaw flexing. "Lucky for me, I have an airtight alibi."

While he turned on the lights, she flung her damp hair over her shoulders and unbuttoned her trench coat. "Clearly there's something more you want to say?"

Texas landscapes lined the walls of the corridor, one end leading to a washroom and the other leading into the house. He eyed her for a moment, sizing her up before nodding tightly. "Your father has led a cutthroat life in the business world. Sterling Perry may not be guilty of this, but the man he has been made it easier to believe it could be him."

She couldn't deny the truth in that. But that was still her daddy Jesse was talking about. "You certainly know how to win friends and influence people."

Sighing, he swept off his hat. "Ma'am, you're clearly tired. I'll make you something to drink—decaf coffee? Tea? Hot chocolate?"

She was exhausted. But she had a narrow window of time. If she kept bristling this way, she would lose the chance to plead her father's case to be the president of the Houston branch of the club. It was tough enough already with all the politics back home, given the other contender for the position was his longtime rival, Ryder Currin, who her father felt had unjustly gotten an oil-rich piece of land that should have stayed in the family. It didn't seem to matter to Sterling that he already had more money than royalty and that Ryder had made the bulk of his fortune through savvy investments.

Although they had to get along these days since Ryder was seeing her sister Angela, that didn't change the fact that her dad wanted the position. And Angela would have to live with that, because Esme intended to make this happen for her father.

"Hot chocolate, please, if it's not too much trouble." It sounded like something that would take longer to make. Give her more time to collect herself. Mold herself into the perfect influencer. "And no worries. I'm thick-skinned like my father."

A fib. She actually was the most sensitive of her siblings, but that would smooth things over for now.

As the sensitive sibling, she'd learned early how to play family peacekeeper. To de-escalate tension and defuse situations—even though her heart often thudded loudly in her chest and panic rose in her blood.

With footfalls uncharacteristically silent for such a tall, broad-chested man, he moved into the laun-

dry room. Light flickered on, and Esme peered inside the well-kept pale yellow room with green plant
accents. He pulled clothes out of a basket on top of
the dryer, then strode with cowboy swagger back
to her. He motioned down the hallway. Sconces on
the wall provided a warm light as they made their
way to the massive kitchen. He placed the neatly
folded clothes on the island.

With a surveying glance, she took in the open,
sprawling layout. White granite countertops provided a sleek contrast to the dark wood cabinets.
Open shelves displayed simple white dishes and
mugs. A countertop overlooked a large bay window
that, despite the night storm raging outside, offered
an enviable view of the large barn and fence. Un-
like the interior of the house, the barn and fence
sported twinkling Christmas lights.

A thick but unfinished sandwich took up the ma-
jority of a white plate on the countertop. He must
have been eating there when he'd spotted her car
outside.

Jesse's rough-cut smile lit up his green eyes.
"Good, I'm glad to hear you're tough. If we're going
to be trapped here together until the road's cleared,
it will be easier if we get along."

Trapped? Now, that sounded promising.

"True enough." She slid off her trench coat.

The room went silent as his eyes flickered with

awareness, taking in her damp blouse and slacks.
Her chilled skin warmed at his gaze.

Then he looked away, clearing his throat as
he picked up a remote control off the island and
thumbed on the sound system. Holiday tunes played
softly, jazz renditions. That surprised her. She
would have expected him to pick country music.

Rubbing the back of his neck, he walked over to
the double wooden doors of his pantry. Intricately
carved, the wood depicted a rearing horse on a landscape. It was a touch of personality in this state-
of-the-art kitchen that was otherwise pretty much
devoid of personality. He removed a bag of marsh-
mallows and a mason jar filled with hot chocolate
mix and set them on the counter. He pulled out milk
from the fridge.

"Well, then, Esme, let's agree not to talk about
your father." He spun a pan in his hand, setting it
down on the front right burner.

Not discussing her dad was rather counterpro-
ductive to her reason for braving the storm to see
him. But she wasn't going to argue with him. She
would work her way back to the subject when the
opportunity arose.

"Fair enough." And while she waited, she
couldn't resist asking, "Let's start with who you
were expecting."

"Actually, three someones." The milk simmered
on the gas stove.

He reached up to the open shelves, selecting an oversize mug. His hands were calloused and capable, telling a story. He didn't just own this massive spread. He worked it.

Surprise lit through her. "Three people you didn't know and wouldn't recognize?"

So…mystery *women*. What was this man up to?

Jesse had maneuvered to a well-stocked bar next to the stainless steel fridge. She noticed a sole picture beside it—of a girl in her twenties who shared his intense green eyes. A sibling perhaps? It was the first—and only—sign of personal effects she'd spotted since entering his ranch house/mansion. A private man, then.

He held up a bottle of peppermint schnapps and quirked an inquiring eyebrow. She nodded and he set the bottle on the counter beside the rest of the ingredients.

"In my defense, Esme, it was dark when I found you and you were—*are* drenched. Speaking of which, you should change before you catch a cold. Your hot chocolate will be ready soon." He stood toe to toe, the spicy and damp scent of him teasing her senses. He passed over the stack of clothes— sweats, a tee and socks—his calloused knuckles brushing hers. "I'll tell you all about the three mystery women when you get back."

Her hands still tingling from the light touch, she sure hoped her father appreciated her efforts here.

Because she suspected focus on her task was going to be tough to come by with Jesse Stevens.

She wasn't even one day into this promotional excursion and already she'd made a mess of things. One that not even the longest, steamiest of showers could make right.

Esme was no stranger to luxury, but she still appreciated the plush robe and heated floors in the guest bathroom he led her to.

An all-Texas bathroom for sure, with a touch of modern rustic charm in the form of the polished horns on the wall opposite the luxurious Jacuzzi. But there was also a large tinted window that offered a view of the Christmas lights lining the fence. The only other lights came from a bunkhouse in the distance.

Under this roof, she was alone. With Jesse Stevens.

Exhaling hard, she plucked one of the lotions from the basket on the counter. She opened the top and inhaled the delicious scent of peppermint, which reminded her of that spiked cocoa waiting for her. Along with the man.

Smoothing the lotion onto her legs, she found her thoughts drifting back to Jesse. His broad shoulders. His blond hair spiked and mussed. Her skin tingled from more than the minty cream.

She'd never doubted her professionalism. Her

cool head. And while she worked for the family company, she'd allowed this to become too personal. This wasn't even about the business. This was about her father's quest to be the president of a club. Which many would have thought meant she was doing a favor, not a job.

Many would be wrong. This was more than a favor. She was trying to earn her dad's approval. Even knowing that shouldn't matter so much to her, an adult woman, she couldn't dodge the truth.

She risked a glance in the mirror. With her hair wet and snarled, she was a mess. A far cry from how she'd started the morning with a spa day. Even her manicure hadn't survived, one nail broken and two others chipped.

It was almost comical, really, as if all her professional facade had been wiped away. Her slacks were ruined. Her silk blouse very likely unsalvageable, too.

All that was left of the real her were her champagne-colored satin underwear and her diamond stud earrings.

At least she had something to wear other than the robe. She stepped into the baggy sweatpants, then the Texas A&M pullover, the fabric warm and tantalizing against her bare skin. She tugged on the athletic socks, bunching them around her ankles. A far cry from the heels she'd slipped on this morning with such relish. But as least she was warm. And clean.

She left the steam-filled bathroom and returned to her suite. Swiping her phone from the coffee table, she dropped down into the desk chair next to the fireplace. Stones flanked the fireplace, giving the guest suite the feel of a swanky cabin. Her toes sank into the plush rug as she FaceTimed her sister.

Of all of her siblings, Angela Perry worried the most. And judging by the four texts Esme had received while she was showering, her sister was imagining every worst-case scenario.

She propped the phone against a leather-bound book on the desk to free her hands to brush through the rat's nest that had replaced her hair.

Within a few rings, her sister's blond hair and rounded face came into view. Angela sat on the ground in front of the new gas fireplace she'd just had installed, flames flickering. Orchestral carols played softly in the background.

"Well, hello there." Angela stared back at her, her blue eyes flaring in surprise. "You look…not like yourself. No offense meant."

"None taken." Running the brush through a knot in her hair, Esme laughed lightly. Her sister had never been a clotheshorse, preferring an understated style. A love of fashion had been at least one thing Esme could share with Melinda, since Angela and her twin had just about everything else in common.

They even lived in the same condominium building—an upscale thirty-two-floor limestone high-rise with wraparound windows and expansive views. The twins had even chosen the same layout, Angela on the fifteenth floor and Melinda on the twenty-fourth.

"Well, this has been quite a day. Or night, rather."

Angela tossed a scrap of Christmas wrapping paper into the fire behind her, then reached for another roll. "Definitely not the image of my glamorous sister."

"Stranger things have happened." But heat still stung her cheeks. One of the ways Esme gained her confidence—and kept her sensitive soul in check—was through a careful curation of makeup, hair and luxurious clothes. The oversize sweats she was wearing rattled her. Threw her off-balance.

Though, if she were being honest, not any more than her sexy host.

Her sister's thin fingers moved deftly over a small stack of jewelry boxes with elegant silver script reading "Diamonds in the Rough." Esme guessed the packages were for her and Melinda, not that she could see inside. Most likely Melinda's contained something to celebrate her baby on the way. The pregnancy had been a surprise to Melinda and her new husband, Slade, but a welcome one. And pregnancy hadn't slowed down her sister's philanthropic works one bit.

To her right, Angela had a bin filled with gold and red foil paper with intricate bows. Designer-level gift-wrapping supplies. A small stack of already-wrapped presents glistened in the fire glow. Esme always told her sister they could afford to pay someone to wrap the gifts for them, but Angela insisted she enjoyed doing it herself, making each one a work of art.

And Christmas was all the more special since Angela had reunited with her former fiancé, Ryder Currin.

Angela ripped clear tape off to secure the golden foil on one of the smaller jewelry boxes. "I'm glad you called. I was starting to get worried. Weather reports are looking terrible in Royal."

Esme thought of the soaked, muddy clothes she had carefully placed in a bag next to the bathtub. She winced a little. "The reports are accurate."

"But you're okay?" her sister asked, genuine worry in her voice.

She nodded, enjoying the soft sounds of violins surging through "Ave Maria."

"I got caught in a flash flood, but lucky for me, I was close to Stevens's ranch. He saw my headlights and came to my rescue."

"Sounds like a close call. I can't imagine your low-slung car held up well in those conditions."

"You can get the judgy tone out of your voice. I know you weren't a fan of my purchase." Esme worked the last of the tangles from her hair, smoothing the brush down the length until she was satisfied that all the knots were out. At least she'd managed to restore some semblance of order in her life.

"It's your money to do with as you please," her sister said as she reached toward a stack of unwrapped presents. Picking up a handsome brass shaving kit, she started sizing up the necessary material to wrap it.

"Well, you can rest easy. My next purchase will come with four-wheel drive." Sporty four-wheel drive.

Angela set down the paper and peered into the screen, her blue eyes fixed but still kind. The look of an older sister. "I just care about you."

"I know." It was tough to discard the defensiveness sometimes, feeling like an outsider with her sisters' twin bond. "And thank you for caring."

Her sister nodded, continuing her methodical wrapping. Without looking up from lining up the edge of the paper with machinelike precision, she said, "So, what's the progress with Jesse Stevens?"

"I've barely had time to shower, much less make progress."

"Shower?" She raised a blond eyebrow. "At Jesse Stevens's house? You're there now?"

"Yes, and no need to sound scandalized. I was drenched. I needed to change." She glanced down at her clothes. When was the last time she'd worn sweats? High school maybe. Or middle school. As rarely as she could manage. "But enough about me. How was your date with Ryder last night?"

Her sister had been engaged to none other than their father's longtime nemesis Ryder Currin, who also happened to be in the running to head the Houston branch of the Texas Cattleman's Club. Angela and Ryder had broken up, but were now back together again with Sterling Perry's blessing. Esme would wager money a reengagement wasn't too far off.

She just hoped Ryder was really right for her sister. He'd been married twice before—divorced from the first wife and widowed by the second. He had one child from each of those marriages, plus an adopted daughter. All adults. Such a complicated blended family.

Angela deserved to have a man love her unconditionally.

"I never thought he and I would have another chance, but things are good, really good."

Her blue eyes turned wistful and the smile that warmed her face drew a pang of guilt from Esme over her doubts and concerns.

"I wish I could have been there for us to talk all about it in person over lunch."

Angela nodded, her smile still present but soft. "That would have been fun, but I understand."

Her sister leaned back to the pile of gifts—a cashmere scarf, leather-bound books, artisanal reclaimed-wood trays. The silver strands in her chunky gray sweater glimmered.

Christmas was coming at the end of the month and Esme hadn't even begun her shopping. She wished she had her sister's love for organization and gift-giving. Maybe then she would feel more connected to the holiday. "If only I'd waited to leave…"

"Dad appreciates what you're doing for him. This is important."

Was it, though? More important than being with her sister? She'd tried to convince her dad that this could wait a couple of days, but he'd insisted. And she hadn't stood up to him. She'd even had the weather as an excuse and she hadn't taken it.

"Well, I'll be back in Houston before you know it. We can have brunch and chat over mimosas."

"That would great. Just let me know when you're finished there and I'll line it up with Melinda, too. We'll definitely need to make it brunch and not breakfast, since Melinda still gets morning sickness." She chewed her fingernail thoughtfully, then added, "Perhaps we could include Tatiana, as well, if you don't mind."

Esme bit her lip to keep from blurting how she wanted to do things on her own with Angela, without their sister, much less Angela's bestie, Tatiana Havery.

Tatiana, a vice president at Perry Holdings who specialized in real estate, had been going through a tough time ever since it came out that Willem Inwood was her estranged half brother. And now that he'd been arrested last week? It would be petty to exclude her.

"Mimosa brunch with you, Melinda and Tatiana. Count on it. Maybe we should invite Ryder's two daughters. I could get to know my future nieces better." She chuckled at the irony of that, since Ryder's daughters were both adults. There was an age gap between Ryder and Angela, but since her sister didn't mind, then who was Esme to judge?

"Okay, then. I will." Angela fluffed her golden-blond hair, surveying the mess of ribbon and foil paper strips around her. "All right, sis, I need to clean up this mess. Thank you for checking in. Please stay in touch."

"I will, just as soon as I have something to report." Esme waved before signing off.

Sighing, she swept her hair into a loose topknot. Casual glam, she told herself.

Time to face her sexy host and try not to wonder if a kiss from him would taste of peppermint schnapps.

Jesse stared out the kitchen window at the water pooling outside, covering the driveway. As the storm continued to rage, he was glad he'd reached Esme when he did.

No denying it, the woman who'd crashed into his life this evening had made quite an impression. He thought about the way her wet clothes clung to her, outlined her shapely body.

Not that she was his type. Too city. Too polished for a ranch lifestyle. Not that it mattered. He had three potential matches coming to the ranch.

Still, his thoughts drifted to the way her wet hair fell in waves. No. He couldn't deny being intrigued by the woman who was currently cleaning herself up in his shower as the rain pelted down.

In the oversize mug, he stirred the hot chocolate. The mug in his hand had been a gift from his little sister. She'd made it in a pottery class, rightly guessing that something homemade would mean more to him. He could buy anything he wanted.

His sister had a knack. The pottery was expertly crafted. She'd called it part of her robin's-egg collection.

He wasn't an overly sentimental man, and even though he and his sister weren't close, this mug represented his last link to family. To something grounding.

After giving the hot chocolate a final stir, he popped the top of the peppermint schnapps, deciding Esme should be the judge of her alcohol level. He didn't want to pour too much. Who knew what her alcohol tolerance was? And he wasn't one to take advantage. He prided himself on being a man of honor.

And he needed to stay focused on his search for a bride, someone who wanted to share this lifestyle with him and build a family.

He turned back to the kitchen and poured himself a cup of coffee with a shot of whiskey in it. Then settled onto a barstool at the kitchen island where his half-eaten sandwich still waited. Fried steak between two thick slices of Texas toast. He took another bite and washed it down with his spiked coffee, the taste firing through his veins on this damn long day.

As he continued to eat his sandwich to the rhythm of rain and thunder, he reflected on the events of the last hour. Now he regretted calling Esme's family "infamous." The word had a crueler inflection than he had meant. Especially since Esme's father was no longer a suspect in the murder. He understood too well what it felt like to be wrongly accused.

Tearing into another bite of his sandwich, he went over the events of the murder investigation in his mind.

He'd been shocked when he was questioned by keen Houston detective Zoe Warren. All because of an argument he'd had with Vincent Hamm. Someone he'd thought he could count on. His kid sister just graduated with an MBA from one of the top programs in the country. Not only was she his sister and he had a strong sense of family, but his sister was also brilliant, with a sharp mind for business. Jesse had asked Vincent to help get his sister in at Perry Holdings. But Vincent refused to even set up an interview for Janet.

Jesse took another sip of his coffee, still trying to understand why, despite all the favors Jesse had done for him, Vincent wouldn't lift a finger to help.

Rage had filled him. He'd believed the worst of his friend. That a big-city job with a fancy salary at Perry Holdings had gone to Vincent's head. That he'd forgotten who he was. Jesse had responded with anger.

And then, a few weeks after their strange encounter, Vincent Hamm was dead. And not just dead—murdered.

A brief angry voice mail from Jesse to Vincent had turned up in the authorities' investigation. A handful of words. Crazy. But Jesse, ever a rule follower and ever meticulous, had a solid alibi. He'd been three hours away at a cattle auction. His location south of Houston was certifiable, easily tracked through his purchase records and through his hotel visit. Nearly all his time was accounted for. There was no feasible way he could have been the murderer. As a law-abiding man, he'd voluntarily submitted to a lie detector test, which he'd passed. He wanted Vincent's actual killer to be found. Sooner rather than later.

He thumped the edge of his own mug, heat transferring ever so slightly from the ceramic to his fingertips.

Jesse's attention returned to the present as he heard the creak of the guest suite door and soft footfalls on the hardwood floor. Then there she was. Esme Perry.

He stood slowly. Damn.

The mug was no longer the only thing throwing heat in the kitchen.

Esme walked deeper into the kitchen, looking too damn sexy in his Texas A&M sweats. Even wearing his athletic socks bunched down around her ankles, she somehow made it all work into an elegant ensemble right down to her diamond stud earrings.

"Well, Miss Esme, you are definitely unmistakable now," he said, nudging her mug and the bottle of schnapps toward her.

"It's nice to be dry again." She gestured to her wet hair. "At least somewhat." She poured some of the liquor into the mug, stirred thoughtfully. Almost absently.

She lifted the mug to her lips, and he found himself unable to look away, imagining how soft they would be.

"I'm glad to help." He waited for her to sit before

reclaiming his place on the barstool. "Did you reach home to let them know you're okay?"

"I did. Just now. I called my sister Angela. We were talking about plans to meet for brunch." Her delicate nose scrunched with worry. "We haven't had much time to talk lately since she got back together with Ryder."

Everyone in Royal had been blown away at the news when Angela and Ryder had gotten engaged. A Perry and a Currin? Unimaginable. Then they had broken things off, and now were apparently a couple again.

Jesse shook his head. He wanted something more stable in his life. "You and she are close?"

She hesitated for a telling moment. "Angela and Melinda are twins. Then I have a brother, Roarke. We all love one another."

He'd heard the gossip that Roarke was rumored to be Ryder Currin's biological son, rumors so strong they'd taken a DNA test. A test that proved Roarke truly was a Perry. Still, the whole ordeal must have put a strain on their family. "That's not the same as being close."

"The twins are close, and our brother has always gone his own way. He's happy, though, working at Perry Holdings in Houston in a newly formed ethics department. He still does part-time work offering legal, too."

"He sounds like quite the crusading attorney for the underdog. I imagine you're proud of him."

"I am. It wasn't easy for him to find his own path. He and Dad butt heads because our father expected Roarke to go into the family business. But that's enough of our family drama." She shrugged, her hair rippling over her shoulder in a blond waterfall. "So you have siblings?"

Her eyes flickered to the photograph tucked on the marble countertop.

Esme was observant. He'd give her that.

"I have a sister. She's all the family I have left, actually. I thought I was going to lose her not too long ago. Her appendix ruptured and she had to have emergency surgery."

Hospital runs and the smell of antiseptic filled his memory. The bargaining and praying for his sister's life he'd done were still a visceral memory in his stomach.

"I'm so sorry. Is she all right now?"

"She is." He looked at the mug in Esme's hand, thankful for his sister's recovery.

"Thank goodness. Still, that had to have been a scary time for you."

"It was."

Rain continued to fall outside, filling the pause with controlled chaos.

She looked into her mug, swirling the hot chocolate around without meeting his gaze. "Actually, you weren't wrong. My sisters have a special bond. My brother, well, his earlier move to Dallas wasn't all that surprising. Now that he's back, that seems to be changing some. Regardless, I'm still stuck somewhere in the middle. But that's all right. Not everyone has the same relationship."

"You don't sound like it's okay."

She raised an eyebrow in surprise, then took another sip of the hot chocolate as she leaned on the granite countertop. She spread her fingers out wide as if soaking in the cool texture. "About those three someones… I'm dying to know more."

"Dates."

Her eyes went wide, and she inched back. "All three? At the same time?"

"Whoa. It's not what you're thinking." He held up his hands defensively, chuckling. "I signed up for a dating service, a matchmaker. She's lined up a trio of candidates. They were each supposed to come out here individually to meet with me, to see my ranching lifestyle and decide if it's off-putting. It's not for everyone."

Her gaze flickering away at the mention of ranching not being for all, she wriggled her toes in his overlarge socks. "A matchmaker. Seriously?"

"Plenty of people sign up for online services. I opted for the matchmaker because of lack of time." Absolutely the truth. And he found a certain sort of…practicality about having an expert match him with someone with similar interests. It saved time rather than meeting scores of women socially and trusting fate to somehow work out his future.

Her forehead furrowing in confusion, Esme leaned slightly forward. "Why do you want to have a girlfriend if you don't even have time to look for one?"

Well, that was easy enough to answer. "I don't want a girlfriend. I want a wife."

Three

"A wife?" Esme repeated, certain she couldn't have heard him correctly. Hot cocoa cradled in her hand, she studied him through narrowed eyes, but couldn't read if he was serious or not. Which could have something to do with how she kept looking at his impossibly broad shoulders. "You're punking me, aren't you?"

"Not at all." He set his coffee cup aside. "I'm looking for a wife."

A flash of disappointment rippled through her. Silly really, since the last thing she wanted was a rancher. "A wife. Not simply a date. That's just… Well, I'm surprised you're already thinking that far down the road about someone you haven't even met."

He crossed his arms over his chest. "Your shock is a little insulting."

"But you're a man." Her eyes were drawn to his arms before she could stop herself. His muscular arms. Arms that had carried her so effortlessly.

"And that comment is decidedly sexist." His green eyes flashed with heat.

She grabbed her mug quickly. She should probably hush before she alienated him altogether. "I apologize. I only meant it's a leap from first date to the altar."

"Apology accepted." He reached for the refrigerator door, his flannel shirt pulling taut along his muscular chest. "Whipped cream?"

"What?" she asked, startled, her gaze shooting back up to his face.

"For your hot chocolate." He held out a can, pointing in her direction.

Her mind traveled sexy pathways, imagining things they could do with that sweet treat.

"Uh, sure." She reached for the can, spraying a swirl inside her mug, when she really wanted to fill her mouth with the stuff and quench at least one hunger. "Of course, there's no reason in the world why you shouldn't find love."

"I didn't say anything about love," he said in the most logical of voices. "Just marriage."

Again, he'd surprised her. This man wasn't at all what she'd expected from reading about him online before her trip to Royal. "Marriage but no love?"

The thought of that chilled her with memories of her parents' loveless marriage. Too many nights, her mother had cried herself to sleep over her husband's staying late at the office yet again. Esme wanted more for herself than that and felt sorry for anyone willing to settle for less.

"Why not? I have my life in order—this house, the ranch." He ticked off points one finger at a time. "The timing is right for the next step. A wife. Then kids."

He'd laid out the events as matter-of-factly as he'd laid out the ingredients to make her hot chocolate. He'd described the process of creating a family as if he was listing the week's upcoming groceries.

She raised an eyebrow. "Do these three mystery women know they're expected to pop out children right away?"

Esme imagined what his dream woman was like. What she wanted. What would make her forsake the idea of love.

Not that Esme had had a lot of luck in that department. Still, she wasn't giving up on finding love—when the time was right, with the man who was right.

She gulped down more hot cocoa and struggled not to wince as it burned her tongue.

"We all filled out extensive questionnaires. Our wishes for the future are in line."

Well, now, that wasn't subtle at all. "And I'm in the way."

Esme blinked a sting of jealousy. She'd only just met Jesse. And while he was sure one sexy cowboy with his slightly tousled blond hair, she knew better than to assume they were anything more than two very opposite people stuck together riding out a rainstorm.

With precise, athletic footfalls, he made his way over to the window and looked outside into the tempest.

"In this storm, I seriously doubt any of them will be showing up." He turned to her and his gaze held on her upper lip, and she realized she had a hint of whipped cream clinging there.

Jesse returned to her, offering her a napkin. She took it, dabbing her mouth slowly. His eyes flamed hotter and she wondered what it would have been like to let him kiss her upper lip, to taste him in return.

She swallowed hard to will away the sensation. "How do they feel about being a part of this edition of *Catch a Bachelor: Rancher Style*?"

He shot her an amused glance, easing back a step. "This isn't a reality show."

"Of course not." She rolled her eyes, struggling for levity. "No cameras."

He cocked an eyebrow. "And they're coming at different times so they don't cross paths."

"How very…civil." And cold. "How do your brides-to-be feel about this emotionless transaction?"

"To be fair, they know about the process. No one's being deceived."

He leaned against the island, an arm's length away. Esme's eyes drifted to his shiny engraved belt buckle. Snapping her attention back to their conversation, she considered the less robotic aspects of such an arrangement. All likes and dislikes already sorted. Everyone knowing the rules of the game. Everyone understanding expectations, too. No mystery. Nothing as quirky as fate intervening.

That was something, at least. "Glad to hear it."

A slow, disarming grin spread across his face. "Are you interested in joining the process?"

"Whoa, nuh-uh." She held up her hands in protest. "I'm in no hurry to fill a nursery, and I've had enough of ranch living."

He tipped his head to the side, studying her, amusement in his eyes replaced by curiosity. "Yet you grew up on a ranch."

Her childhood home on the outskirts of Houston was a sprawling mansion, almost castle-like, surrounded by pastures, elegant barns. The spread was a huge, billion-dollar cattle-and-horse operation started by her maternal grandfather, then passed on to her parents. And even with all of that, Esme had still moved into the city the first chance she had.

"Exactly. No more ranching for me." And that was all the reminder she needed for why she should keep her distance from this man and stay focused on her reason for being here. "Thank you for the hot cocoa and the clothes and the rescue. I should turn in for the night."

She rinsed her mug and made fast tracks for the guest suite before she was tempted to stay in the kitchen. To listen to the warm timbre of his voice.

To imagine the taste of whiskey from his coffee on his tongue if he kissed her.

Sleep had been a difficult commodity for Jesse, with images of his surprise houseguest filling his dreams. Visions of her soaking wet, yet equally enticing in sweats. What would it be like to peel those clothes from her body?

Restless, he'd finally given up sleep just before dawn and gone to the barn to burn off energy.

His cowboy boots reverberated on the cement floor as he approached Juniper's stall. Grabbing the supple brown leather halter and lead, he made his way into the stall of his newest horse.

Juniper, a young dapple gray mare, stretched her neck, giving her tangled mane a shake. She sniffed his hand, her whiskers softly touching his palm. The horse exhaled warm breath against his fingertips, a welcome sensation in the cool, damp morning air. Stepping closer, Jesse slipped the cognac halter on her head and led the mare to the crossties, where his brushes were waiting for him.

He never grew tired of this, the connection with his horses and the land. Ranching was more than a job to him. It was a way of life.

Picking up a currycomb, he moved his hand in circular patterns. Excess hair and dirt gathered in the brush.

Other horses poked their heads from stalls. The barn held two rows of twelve stalls. Buddy, his first gelding, lazily chewed on hay, dropping bits of straw onto the ground. Flash, a muscular chestnut quarter horse, loosed a whinny. Beneath his hands, Juniper sucked in a breath before belting out an answering noise.

Satisfied, Flash moved back into his well-kept stall.

The routine grounded Jesse, reminding him of his reasons for using the matchmaker for a practical choice.

Practical.

That was the mantra he said to himself as he picked up the hard brush. His hand moved in time to the rain pelting the tin roof.

Images of his sexy houseguest kept interrupting his thoughts. *Practical. Practical. Practical.*

How many times would he need to say that until

it sank into his brain? He surveyed the barn, wondering if he would need to groom every horse today to refocus himself.

Of course, that was the opposite of practical.

After finishing up with Juniper, he led the mare back to her stall and gave her the carrot he'd shoved in his pocket earlier. The mare crunched her treat, flicking her ears forward in something that seemed like thanks.

Latching her stall, he started to leave the barn. He pushed his Stetson down on his head to keep the cold rain from pelting his ears as he made his way back to the ranch house. The cold nipped at his hands as he moved past the pool, his boots trekking through the muddy earth as he closed the distance to the green door of the back entrance. The matchmaking prospects certainly wouldn't be arriving today, or the next, if the weather didn't ease up soon.

After wicking the rain off his Stetson, he hung his hat on a hook and discarded his leather jacket and mud-drenched boots. The hall led to the kitchen, where he found Esme sitting in front of the fireplace in the lotus position. A plated pastry and coffee mug rested on the mahogany end table to her left.

Damn.

His heart hammered.

Hair drawn up into a sleek ponytail and skin

dewy in the firelight, she looked enticing, even in a long slouchy sweater and floral leggings his sister had left behind. Somehow, the pink sweater hinted at her curves, and the floral leggings made her look oddly polished.

His athletic socks still warmed her feet, and he realized he'd have to find her suitable footwear.

Something practical. The word echoed again as he reached for another mug from the open shelf.

"I've had your car towed to my mechanic." He poured himself black coffee, allowing himself to taste the bitter cocoa and fruit undertones. "Carl—who towed your vehicle—said it wouldn't start."

"Oh no, I was afraid of that." She scrunched her nose in dismay. "Because of the flash flood?"

"Most likely." He was drawn to her, this bewitching and beautiful woman. He dropped into the brocade chair on the other side of the fireplace. "If Carl can make it here on his four-wheeler, he'll bring your luggage. Otherwise, you'll have to make do with my sister's clothes for a while longer." He'd offered them to her last night. "I'll see if I can find some rain boots that fit you."

Esme's delicate fingers moved like sultry smoke as she removed her thin phone from where it was tucked under her thigh. "I'll put in a request for a rental car for when the rain lets up. Hopefully they'll have something available."

He stretched his legs out in front of him, powerful legs encased in denim. "You might as well save yourself the time."

"Why?" She hesitated. "Is there a problem?"

"This time of year, with the holidays and all, rentals are all booked for weeks." He flashed her his best bad-boy grin, even though he'd officially hung up his bad-boy ways. "I could lend you a vehicle."

"That would be so helpful." She placed her phone beside her on the armchair. "Thank you."

He watched her through narrowed eyes, unable to resist. "I have an extra truck. It's twenty-two years old, but runs great. Carl's a super mechanic."

She fidgeted with the end of her blond ponytail, rubbing the strands between her fingers, clearly caught off guard by his offer. "Oh, uh, yes, thank you."

He narrowed his gaze, assessing the impossibly posh woman in front of him. "You've never driven one, have you?"

She arched an eyebrow. "Actually, I learned on an ancient stick-shift truck at Daddy's ranch. A Ford so ancient I figured no one would notice if I added an extra dent or two."

"Touché." He lifted his mug, toasting in her direction.

She eyed him intuitively as the flames licked upward in the fireplace. "You were teasing me."

"Perhaps."

She raised a finger to her lips. "Shhhh. Don't tell your three potential brides that."

A begrudging laugh barked free and before he could second guess himself, he said, "Maybe if the rain lets up this afternoon, we'll get enough of a break to chop down a Christmas tree. That is, if you want to come along?"

"Sure," she said, already launching to her feet. "As long as you don't expect me to load it into the truck."

She flashed him a sassy wink.

"You can just stand there and look pretty." And the thing was, he meant it.

So much for keeping his distance. But something about this woman tempted him more than he wanted to admit.

Jesse's flirtatious words still echoed in Esme's ears two hours later. Steering the conversation toward her father and the club was tougher than she'd expected.

But she was determined to keep her cool. Slow and steady was her best option. And thanks to their current project sorting Christmas ornaments while waiting for a break in the rain to get a tree, she would have the time she needed.

Despite the rain, light beamed through the floor-to-ceiling windows on two of the four walls of the great room. That, coupled with the cathedral ceilings, made the petal-white room feel impossibly airy.

Which was good considering all the boxes of Christmas ornaments that flanked the white love seat and leather couch. She'd moved the glass-and-wood table in order to create room for the bins Jesse had brought down from the attic, noting as he did so that these were only the tip of the iceberg.

To set the mood and to gain control, Esme queued up her favorite Christmas playlist from her phone, connecting it to the Bluetooth surround-sound system. A hazy, warbly '50s-era carolers version of "Here We Come A-Wassailing" filled the room.

There.

The start of Christmas. And the real start of her mission.

They opened the first box of ornaments. Reaching into the box, she pulled out two silver bells, one with Jesse's name engraved on it, the other with the name Janet etched on it. "Your sister, right?"

"Yes, we split the decorations between us. Somehow I must have missed giving her that one." His brow furrowed and he tilted his head to the side, inspecting the silver bells. For a moment, she wondered if he'd pull out his phone and snap a picture to send to his sister. But his hands made no move for the phone in his pocket.

"How long until you get to see her over Christmas?" A little prying, but curiosity filled her as she laid the ornaments down with care onto the sofa.

"Like I said, my family wasn't tight-knit," he said, not that it answered her question. "My parents didn't get along. They're gone now." His face hardened, tight lines pulling at the corners of his mouth.

"I'm sorry for your loss. My mother died ten years ago and I still miss her dreadfully." She fidgeted with the thin bracelet her mother had given her so long ago.

Her mom—Tamara—had been a kind and loving mother. Esme knew her parents hadn't married out of romance, and seeing their unhappiness only made her all the more determined not to settle for less than a fully committed heart.

The loss of her mom made Esme cling all the harder to the rest of her family. She couldn't imagine what she would do without them. Her dad and her siblings meant the world to her. Christmases were big, boisterous events for them. Sometimes it had been a challenge to get Roarke to join in, but she and her sisters had worked to wear him down. She had high hopes for him this year, now that he'd found happiness with his new love, Annabel. "That's got to be tough for you and your sister, having lost both parents. I can see how maybe it would have brought you two closer to each other."

She pulled out an ornament tucked in protective

paper. Glitter twinkled as she removed the wrapping to reveal a reindeer towing a sleigh.

"Janet's great, and I do love her, of course. It about killed me to think I might lose her when her appendix burst. But she's well now, thank God." A sigh racked him and he scrubbed a hand over his face.

"That had to be so scary." She stopped unpacking ornaments, searching his face, cradling the sleigh in her hand. "You'll have a lot to celebrate together over Christmas, with her recovery."

He ran his fingers through his blond hair, then rubbed along the back of his neck. "It's unlikely we'll see each other. We don't have much in common. She's a lot younger than I am, and, well, we just have our own lives now."

Jesse looked away and pulled out a snow globe, full of glitter around a tree, a nutcracker and a ballerina. A wistful shadow played across his face.

His thumb stroking the smooth glass, he flipped over the trinket and wound it up. "The Dance of the Sugar Plum Fairy" played as a snowstorm enveloped the little scene.

Biting her lip, she couldn't help but be moved by such a glimpse of nostalgia in this rough-and-tumble man. She stood, reaching a hand to touch his shoulder, then stopping short. "But perhaps the ornaments remind you of happy memories?"

"Yeah, they do." He set the globe on the mantel.

"And I look forward to making memories with my own kids one day."

Well, that was sure a splash of cold water, reminding her of his plans. She pulled a smile and tugged at the hem of the pink sweater. "Your sister has nice taste in clothes."

He angled his head. "Are you being sarcastic, Ms. Prada?"

"It's not office wear, but it's fun for ranch work, soft and cheerful."

"That's nice you can appreciate a less flashy style."

"I'm not a snob." She handed him a longhorn ornament.

"Really?" He took the decoration, their fingers brushing.

Her skin tingled even after he'd pulled away. "You don't have to sound so surprised."

The snow globe stopped playing just as the song drifting through the speakers subsided. For a moment, silence filled the great room.

Desire danced in the air, an electricity between them as he moved closer to her. "Would it soften the sting to your ego if I told you how hot you look no matter what you're wearing?"

Music started on her phone again, orchestral carols stroking the air.

She closed her hand into a fist, trying to will away the lingering sensation of that simple touch.

"And what about those three bridal prospects of yours, one of whom will give you babies to make Christmas memories with?"

He canted back, nodding tightly. "You're right. It's totally inappropriate of me. I mean it when I say I want to be a family man, and all that entails."

"The epitome of a Texas Cattleman's Club fella."

"Yes, exactly that." His gaze held hers, setting her skin on fire with just the stroke of his eyes on her face.

Even knowing it was unwise and there were so many reasons they were wrong for each other, she still felt herself sway toward him. His hand lifted slowly, reaching out to tuck her ponytail back over her shoulder. Then his fingers slid to cup the back of her head. Goose bumps of awareness spread over her and she wanted this moment, this connection. Just one kiss.

With luck, it wouldn't even be a very good kiss and she could refocus on her plans to repair her father's reputation. So giving in to temptation was the right thing to do. Or at least that's what she could tell herself as she angled forward the rest of the way for her lips to meet his.

And damn, it was very far from being a bad kiss.

Four

Jesse had expected the kiss to be good. Esme was a sexy woman, after all.

He had not expected that his senses would be set on fire at the first brush of her lips against his. A connection he fully intended to deepen. And explore.

Sliding his arms around her, he drew Esme to his chest, angling his mouth over hers, his tongue tracing the seam of her lips until they parted and…

Thoughts fled until only sensation remained. The soft give of her breasts against his chest. The glide of her hair through his fingers as he cupped the back of her head. He could smell the scent of shampoo and wondered what perfume she chose. What would be in her suitcase once the weather cleared enough to retrieve it. He wanted to feel and learn more about her. More than just the kiss.

Although it was still one helluva kiss.

She tasted of coffee and mint and something innately *her*.

Music hummed softly in the background and rain came down in sheets outside, all almost drowned out by the hammering of his speeding pulse. A breathy sigh whispered from her and he groaned, surrendering to this moment with her.

He swept a hand behind her, brushing away the ornaments and paper, clearing a space to recline her back in the thick woven rug. Her arms twined around his neck and she arched closer, skimming her mouth over his neck up to nip his earlobe.

Irresistible.

Her breasts pressed against his chest in a sweet temptation, her foot stroking the back of his leg as her thighs parted ever so slightly. He'd wanted her since the first time he saw her on the side of the road. The fierce desire for her swept him away as surely as the storm sweeping over the landscape. Until the power of it was ringing in his ears.

Except…

"Your phone," she gasped softly, her breath warm against his skin. "I think that's your phone ringing."

And it was. The text message sound dinged a couple more times. Each successive ring called him back to reality. And each ring raised the level of surprise more and more of what had just occurred. The surprise of the heat that passed between their bodies.

Damn. How could he have lost control so fully? His focus narrowed sharply as he angled off her, swiping his cell off the coffee table. Multiple texts scrolled across the screen and he cursed under his breath.

"Is something wrong?" she asked, elbowing up, her cheeks flushed, her hair tousled from his hands.

She quickly straightened her clothes. The moment had passed. Even if he could stay. Which he couldn't.

He pocketed his phone. "That was my foreman. He and the rest of my crew are cut off from the barn by the rain. I've got to get to the animals." He paused, stroking a finger down her face lightly. "I'm sorry to leave abruptly."

"It's okay. You're needed," she assured him, smiling but inching back. She crossed her arms somewhat protectively around her stomach and chest, as if she were Alice in Wonderland shrinking before his eyes. "And it's not like the kiss was anything more than an impulsive mistake for both of us."

Ouch. That stung more than a little. Because

as far as he was concerned, it was a steamy, soul-searing kiss that he wouldn't mind repeating.

But she was right. He'd had no business losing control with her. "If you need anything, call me." He pulled a card from his wallet and passed it over quickly. "All right? Promise?"

"Absolutely." She eased to her feet, backing away. "I should call my sister and check in again anyway." She turned from him, her sun-gold hair glistening.

He reached for her hand, stopping her, not sure what he planned to say until the words fell out of his mouth. "That kiss may have been a mistake, but I don't regret it for a second."

Hoping her distraction didn't show, Angela Perry half listened to her sister Esme's latest check-in call from Royal while staring out at the Houston skyline from her high-rise condominium. At least they weren't FaceTiming today, so any distraction wouldn't be visible. Esme was going on and on about decorating with Jesse, down to what his decorations looked like.

And yes, Angela was more than ready to embrace the Christmas season, all the way down to the tree behind her with freshly wrapped gifts. She'd had one helluva tough year, caught in the middle of the feud between her father and Ryder Currin.

Maybe that was a part of why she was having trouble mustering too much enthusiasm for Esme's call.

Their father's latest ploy to become the president of the Houston branch of the Texas Cattleman's Club was frustrating. Ryder certainly wasn't using a PR expert to sway votes.

Worry gnawed at Angela over what might happen if her father lost. Would he withdraw his recently extended blessing over her dating Ryder again?

A roll of nausea rippled through her. Pain, recent and still tender, colored her memories. Breaking off the engagement had just about broken her heart—and his. Taking a risk on becoming a couple again had been scary.

Though she knew Ryder was her future, emotions still ran high. Angela chewed the inside of her lip, a habit she picked up as a child when nerves got the best of her during school competitions or when she needed an anchor back to the world. Not that this was the best way to cope.

But it was a way.

And she sure as hell needed something right now.

"Angela?" Her sister's voice snapped her out of her reverie. "I'm rambling, aren't I?"

"Not at all," Angela lied, more than aware of how Esme sometimes felt excluded by her sisters. Angela loved both of her sisters, but in her heart of hearts, she knew there was a difference with her twin bond to Melinda. Not that she would ever admit as much to Esme. "I appreciate your checking in and I'll be sure to pass along the update to the rest of the family."

"Thank you. I hope I have something more concrete to share before long."

Hearing Ryder stirring about in the kitchen, Angela figured she'd better cut this conversation short before her sister freaked out that something may have been overheard. "Stay safe and good luck with Jesse Stevens."

She signed off just as Ryder stepped from the kitchen into the living room, carrying a wooden tray of meats, cheeses and olives. He was such a wonderful man. And sexy.

If she didn't already know him, she would have never guessed he had three adult children. Like Brad Pitt, Ryder looked better and better with age.

Even in faded blue jeans and a chambray shirt, Ryder looked like he'd stepped off some movie set. Short, dark blond hair framed his tanned face. Blue eyes as bright as a Texas summer sky met her gaze, just as warm as a summer day, too.

As he yawned, his square, cut jawline moved. Even in these little gestures, he was handsome. He stretched, walking toward her in socks. His well-worn brown boots still took up residence by the fireplace.

Theirs had a been rocky relationship, made more

than a little difficult since their families had been bitter rivals for years. Ryder had been a lowly ranch hand on the ranch outside Houston where Sterling Perry—an old-money Houston heir—was briefly the foreman during his engagement to Harrington York's daughter.

As part of a business and social alliance, Harrington had offered his daughter Tamara's hand in marriage to Sterling Perry, as long as Sterling agreed to learn the ranch business from the inside and then live there after he married. When Harrington had died, Sterling had seen Ryder comforting Tamara and assumed they were having an affair, even though Tamara was a decade older.

Discovering that Harrington had willed a key piece of oil-laden land to Ryder had only added fuel to fire, even though Sterling had inherited the bulk of the estate. When over two decades later, Ryder and Angela became an item, Sterling had been enraged. His fury had led to Angela and Ryder breaking up. Finding their way back together had been a long, heartbreaking journey.

But here they were, trying again with the hope of the Christmas season urging them on.

"You're so thoughtful." She extended her legs, wriggling her toes in front of the fire. The rain was making even a Texas winter cold. "I'm starving."

His gaze lingered on her legs for a second beyond casual interest before he set the tray on the end table and sat beside her, his jeans and chambray shirt covering those honed muscles of his. "How's your sister doing?"

Thinking back to the drawn-out conversation with Esme, she tilted her head from side to side. "She's still flooded in at Jesse Stevens's place."

She decided he didn't need to hear all about the decorations.

"Well, I guess that's convenient for your father."

She struggled to hide a wince, concern firing anew. "Please don't say you mean that in a negative way."

He held up his hands, his blue eyes widening. "I get that your dad wants to be the president of the new Texas Cattleman's Club chapter. And we all know that your father can be…determined when he sets his mind to something. Just look at how hard he pushed to break us up."

Angela's mouth tightened at the truth of his words.

However, it hadn't helped that an executive at Ryder's oil corporation had been the one spreading rumors about her father and a Ponzi scheme that had almost destroyed Perry Holdings.

Bringing that up wouldn't be wise at the moment. So she settled on, "But my father relented about us."

"You're right." Shifting his weight, he leaned toward her. "Then he promptly sent your sister to

Royal to tip the scales in his favor," he added, his face showing lines of stress and concern.

"It's not like he sent her to seduce Jesse. She's a highly qualified PR executive."

"She's a daddy's girl," he muttered. His jaw became rock solid. Tense.

"And your daughters aren't?" Angela knew otherwise. Both girls loved their dad. And he loved them. He was so proud of Annabel's makeover business, Fairy Godmother. And Maya, his adopted daughter. Things had been in turmoil with them since Maya had demanded more information on her birth parents. But the eighteen-year-old had never doubted her dad's love.

Angela chewed on her lip until she tasted iron. She felt her stomach knotting. "You and my father have hated each other for a long time. I know that's not going to magically go away just because you and I are an item. I only want the two of you to try."

"He and I have come to a truce—"

"It feels more like a temporary cease fire."

A wry grin tucked into his face. "For your sake, we're offering a united, powerful front to get to the bottom of what's going on."

"And after that's been solved?" She didn't want to think about losing Ryder or her father.

"Well, one of us is going to be leading the new chapter. If it's him, I'll be polite. If it's me…?"

She didn't want any part of this conversation

anymore. And she had a damn good idea of how to distract them both. She angled toward him, smoothing the collar of his chambray shirt. "Let's stop talking about my father."

"Sure. If you're done with this—" he gestured to the tray of snacks "—then we can head out to finish up the last of your shopping. Although I can't imagine you have more to buy."

"Or we could skip the shopping." She shifted to straddle him, tugging at his shirt.

Grin kicking up the sides of his mouth, he cupped her hips, his eyes smoldering. "Excellent idea."

After her phone call with Angela, Esme had grown restless. It hadn't escaped her notice that her sister sounded breathless and a bit distracted. Ryder Currin's fault, no doubt.

She was happy for her sister, but also concerned for her dad. He was getting older, and this club presidency meant the world to him.

Determined not to waste time, she'd finished getting dressed in clothes left behind by Jesse's sister. She'd even managed to find a pair of rain boots that fit if she put on three pairs of socks. At the thought of seeing her handsome host, her nerves pattered as fast as the rain.

Yesterday she would have sworn she wouldn't be venturing out into the rain again anytime soon. And here she was, pushing out of the door and running through the storm in an oversize slicker that wasn't much more attractive than the sweats she'd worn last night.

Sure, he could most certainly handle things in the barn on his own, but he had saved her. And kissed her.

Who was she trying to kid?

She wanted to spend more time with him. To persuade him for her dad and because he was an interesting, charismatic man. She couldn't remember when she'd been this drawn to anyone this quickly.

She wanted to see if the chemistry of that kiss had been a fluke.

A well-appointed barn stood guardian before a small patch of trees. As the cold rain continued to pelt down, she widened her stride and dashed for the door.

Once her boots crossed the threshold, she whisked the rain off her body. Drips melted into the floor as her breath slowed. Then she quieted to watch Jesse, unnoticed for the moment.

Hands wringing her damp hair, Esme held her breath as Jesse's muscled form gently stroked a bay horse. Even from a few feet away, she saw the whites of the horse's eyes and the flaring nostrils.

Something had spooked the bay, who kept tossing his head skyward on the crossties, front hooves picking up and down as if he might bolt. Jesse's practiced hand stroked the horse's neck as he spoke impossibly softly in an attempt to soothe the still-frightened animal.

Electricity danced in the air again. Sure, she hadn't anticipated being drawn to him at all. The kiss from earlier drifted back into her mind as this softer-but-still-powerful Jesse filled her vision.

As if sensing her, the bay craned his neck around, nostrils flaring once again, scenting her. Jesse was alerted to her presence and turned around.

"Well, hello, I didn't expect to see you out here. In case you hadn't noticed, there's a crazy-strong storm raging out there."

Grinning, she hung up the slicker on an empty peg along the wall. "I did notice, thank you, and it seemed to me that perhaps you could use some help."

He angled his head to the side, studying her through narrowed eyes. "You realize this isn't glamorous, right?"

"I know what I'm getting in for. I grew up on a ranch, something you seem to keep forgetting. Just because I don't choose to continue that way of life doesn't mean I magically forgot all I learned." Her arms folded across her chest.

"Okay, then," he conceded. "I welcome the extra set of hands. Especially ones so knowledgeable."

She took that as a challenge. A half smile tugging on her lips, she raised a brow. "Point me in the direction of what still needs accomplishing."

After he'd given her a quick rundown of what he'd done thus far—currycombing, hard brush and soft brush on Ace, the bay on the crossties—he launched into how the bay needed to have his hoof wrapped to deal with an abscess.

Reaching back over a decade, Esme remembered when her own buckskin mare had abscessed. If she were being honest, the flow of the care stayed with her but the particulars faded into the background.

Approaching the horse, she offered the palm of her hand to Ace. Sniffing gingerly, the horse's whiskers tickled her palm. But he visibly settled, a great sigh releasing the tightness in his neck. The crossties hung in loose loops for the first time.

"You're a natural." Jesse's eyes showed surprise as she stroked the horse's leg, feeling for the heat of the infection.

Warmth danced on her cheeks, but she willed a casual wink to keep her mind off how close her body was to Jesse's. "Sometimes I get lucky."

Standing up, she looked at the supplies he'd gathered. He bent over, asking the horse to raise the injured foot with a click of his tongue and a tap on the ankle bone. Ace, shifting his weight, complied.

Eyeing the pile, she recognized the Betadine bottle and handed it to him.

"So the city girl does remember her origins after all." He laughed, cradling the hoof as he poured the antiseptic on it.

His muscles rippled with a strength that took her breath away. Which was especially impressive given that she'd spent her life around cowboys, had seen plenty. But he was in a class of his own.

He was more than a figurehead ranch owner.

"Just here for the assist. What is the next step? I'm afraid this is where it gets fuzzy for me."

Looking up from the hoof, he smiled, nodding toward the supply bucket. "I need a pad and tape."

She nodded, handing him the last bit he needed to ensure the horse would heal properly. While he wrapped the horse's hoof, she spoke quietly to Ace, stroking his silky neck until the horse's eyes became heavy.

He finished checking his medical work and then carefully placed the wrapped hoof down. In a fluid movement, he snapped the lead line onto the leather halter and unhooked the crossties. Leading Ace back to his stall, he fished a treat out of his pocket, which the horse happily munched.

After closing the stall door, Jesse led her down the aisle to the wooden door of the barn office. The space was lit by overhead lighting and a blinking Christmas tree in the corner near a sturdy wood desk, scarred from use and full of papers. It had a different vibe than the expertly decorated house and pristine horse stalls. And how ironic that he'd put a Christmas tree in here, but not in his home yet.

She wondered if this might be a peek into his

core personality, less constrained, less intent on being analytically perfect in his approach to everything.

He opened a stainless steel refrigerator tucked behind the desk and pulled out two water bottles, one for each of them.

Extending one bottle to her, he leaned on the desk's edge. "Did you reach your sister?"

"I did. You probably think it's strange how often she and I talk—given that you said you're not close to Janet."

"I think if you're both happy with your relationship, then that's awesome." He gestured for her to sit in the leather office chair. "I wish I'd had a houseful of siblings."

"And that's why you've got these three blind dates coming to meet you," she said, trying very hard not to notice how amazing the chair smelled, carrying the hint of him in the leather, like being wrapped in his arms.

"That's the plan." He shook his head wryly. "You were *not* a part of my plan."

"Sorry?"

"I'm not," he said enigmatically, continuing before she had a chance to question him. "You were incredible in there with the horses. Thank you, Esme."

She fidgeted with the bracelet on her wrist. The one from her mom that she couldn't ever remember being without. A small fidget of comfort. "I only did what was needed."

"But you *knew* what was needed, sometimes before I had a chance to ask. That's impressive." He nodded. "Yes, I know. You grew up on a ranch, but not everyone pays attention. And it's not as if you needed to work."

Helping on the ranch had been yet another way she'd tried to impress her father, only to see he hadn't noticed because, to her surprise, he didn't like the lifestyle. He didn't even like horses, which blew her away because even the city girl in her loved the horses.

All the same, here she was again, still trying to prove she was indispensable. "What's going to happen with the Houston chapter of the Cattleman's Club?" she asked, blurting out what was on her mind.

"I can't predict the election," he said noncommittally.

"Do you think my dad has a chance?" Was she wasting her time here? What if Jesse said no and she would have to leave the second the rain stopped?

"Sure, he has a chance."

"But so does Ryder Currin."

He shrugged.

She sighed, the truth slipping out, frustration and fear of failure weakening her defenses. "I wish someone else was running. If Dad's going to lose, it's going to be so much tougher for him to swallow seeing Ryder at the helm."

"I thought they'd reconciled."

Had she said too much? Would that ongoing battle be a problem for the charter chapter? "They're making an effort for my sister. But they've hated each other for a long time. It's tough to believe they once worked together."

Except her father had known he would marry his boss's daughter. Which was ironic since her father didn't even enjoy ranching, not the way Jesse did. The way Ryder Currin did, too, for that matter.

All a moot point. Her father would make a good president for the new club. Winning would also make it much easier for her dad to accept Ryder with Angela.

And if her dad knew the turn things had taken with Jesse Stevens and that kiss?

Even the word flamed through her, leading her gaze to slide back to Jesse. His eyes met hers quizzically, then knowingly. Heat glinted in his expression.

The air crackled with awareness between them and she couldn't will herself to break away. The tip of her tongue moved over her top lip in an unconscious invitation.

Still seated on the edge of the desk, Jesse angled toward her, his hand sliding to cup the back of her neck. He angled his mouth over hers, and desire radiated through her, driving her to her feet. She looped her arms around his neck and held him close, and somehow, it wasn't nearly close enough. She ached for more of him, all of him. She couldn't stop the sigh of desire from escaping her lips.

A low rumble of pleasure vibrated his chest against hers a second before he swept his arm across his desk. Binders crashed to the floor, papers fluttering before they fell to rest. His arms hooked under her bottom, lifting her and setting her on the sleek mahogany surface.

Surprise flickered through her, excited her, spurred her to demand more, to throw caution to the wind and see how far they could take things. An invitation he seemed to understand, since he lowered her against the desk, then lay over her.

Her world narrowed to the music of the moment.

Her heart hammering in her ears.

Rain drumming on the roof.

A car roaring up the drive…

A car?

She froze, her skin chilling with realization. Jesse angled back, his head turning, his brow furrowed. He started toward the window and she bolted to her feet, making it there only a step behind Jesse.

An SUV was racing up the drive, rainwater sloshing from behind the speeding vehicle all the way to the front porch. She took one look at the sensible four-wheel drive with a cowgirl-hat-wearing woman stepping out from behind the wheel, and Esme knew.

In spite of the weather, the first of those match-making candidates had arrived.

Five

In all of his imaginings, this was not how he'd anticipated meeting his potential future bride. With the taste of another woman still on his lips, the exotic scent of her clinging to his shirt.

Papers were strewn all over the floor because he'd been a heartbeat away from taking Esme right here, right now, on his desk. Practical plans for his future be damned.

Jesse scrubbed a hand over his face, exhaling hard over the latest arrival. He should be relieved. The woman pulling up to the house could be his wife one day. According to the matchmaker, he had one in three odds this was it.

Yet Jesse couldn't help but be frustrated over her timing. He'd been enjoying the afternoon with Esme. She'd surprised him again today. Not just with showing up to help, but by being completely unaffected by mud and dung and hard work. He couldn't deny he'd been very impressed. But he also knew he couldn't fall for her. She was all about her job, her glamorous lifestyle, and didn't seem the least bit interested in marriage and children. Or so it appeared from the way she'd reacted to him saying that's what he wanted, his reason for reaching out to the matchmaker.

"Well," Esme said, backing away from the window, rain boots squeaking on the floor with a reminder of all her help, "this is awkward."

Her husky voice turning airy, he could feel the attempt at humor and he appreciated the effort to downplay the situation. But it didn't alleviate it enough.

And it wasn't going to get easier.

He looked out the window at the newcomer again. Given the number of paw print stickers on her back window, he guessed, "That must be Amaryllis Davis. She's a veterinarian, only lives about an hour away."

"Amaryllis? Her name is Amaryllis?" Esme bit her bottom lip for a moment, scrunching her nose before continuing, "Forget I said that. My name's

Esme, for goodness' sake. I have no room to tease anyone over what a mama chooses for a name."

He knew he should say something to smooth over this moment, but he didn't have a clue. Never could he have imagined himself in this position. "I'm sorry about the timing."

It was probably the lamest sentence he could offer her. But no other words formed. Comforting her with his touch would cross a line. Again. And he knew he needed to reel back his emotions. Tuck them away. Focus on the future. On finding his perfect mate.

"You were honest from the start about the match-making prospects." Her beautiful face tensed into unreadable lines. She shook her head, honey-blond hair rippling in the office light.

He stared at her for a handful of heartbeats. Not long really, since his pulse was racing from being near Esme. It was so damn wrong that he wanted to steal one last kiss from her. That he was wondering what might have happened if he'd met Esme before contacting that matchmaker.

Those thoughts weren't fair to Esme or the woman outside. Or the other two candidates on the way.

Still, he had trouble shutting them down.

With his current luck, they would probably show up early, too.

Esme inched back a step, increasing the distance between them. "You should go meet her without me.

I'll just hang here and text my sister." She waved him off like it was no big deal, but her eyes told another story. "I need to firm up plans to meet my sisters for brunch with Angela's friend Tatiana."

"You're sure?" he asked one last time. "We'll talk as soon as... Well, once we see if she's staying or not. You aren't going to leave yet, are you?"

A hopeful question. One he shouldn't ask. One he had to. He straightened the papers on his desk and picked up the binders, looking up at her.

Slender hands twirled her long blond hair. He noticed her chipped manicure. She cleared her throat. "I don't have a car and I'm guessing you didn't leave the keys in the old truck."

Her levity during an awkward moment just made her all the more appealing. And he'd only known her for a day. He told himself it was infatuation. Chemistry. Not the stuff practical unions were made of.

Looking down at the scattered ranch documents, he knew the more practical path was the path that continued forward with his plan. Secure a woman who shared his goal to raise a family. Someone who believed in the legacy he wanted to build.

Steeling his resolve, he nodded and turned to leave. To meet the woman the matchmaker had called his 98 percent perfect mate.

Grudges were a bitch. And she knew that better than most. Even if she kept a smile on her face so that no one would guess the person behind all the Perry and Currin grief was actually a woman.

How sexist of them to keep assuming only a man could take them down.

She sat at the conference table in Perry Holdings headquarters in Houston and knew she should be content. Happy even. Her job here at Perry Holdings gave her the money and prestige she'd burned for as a child growing up in poverty.

Listening to all of these entitled blue bloods at work made her blood boil with resentment over all they took for granted. Hearing them bandy about plans to spoil their children at Christmas with extravagant gifts and vacations reopened old wounds and depthless anger. It took all her theater training from college to keep her face neutral. To check the fire that burned in her chest. That resentment had become unbearable when she'd learned how the Perrys and Currins had cheated her out of a chance for a better life.

She eased back in the massive conference chair, the offices radiating the aura of elegance-meets-the-West. Perry Holdings had four floors in a downtown Houston skyscraper. But this could have been her father's business, his success. His *power*.

Or Currin Oil, with its five floors in an elegant brick office building in a more industrial neighborhood on the outskirts of Houston. At least the meeting was finally shifting from discussion of buying diamond earrings for a baby to starting the business meeting.

Such as it was.

Schooling her face to feign interest in the outrageously long discussion about the recent fluctuation in stock prices, she drummed her fingers impatiently along her leg under the table. Bracketed by Ethan Barringer and Roarke Perry, she hoped they wouldn't notice her nerves. She worked to ground herself by fingering the texture of her Chanel linen business suit, the hem just grazing the top of her knees. None other than her boss, Sterling Perry, led the meeting. He was so arrogant, all smiles now that the cloud of suspicion had shifted from him.

But she wasn't surrendering. Not yet. Not ever.

Understanding about the detriment of grudges didn't stop the burning need to take down everyone in the Perry and Currin families. And they had no idea how close danger had been, still was. They were all so damned arrogant that way. They didn't understand what it was like to grow up a joke, her status always one giant step behind that of her so-called friend.

And now, here she sat, right under Sterling Perry's unsuspecting nose.

He was so arrogant, so full of himself in his expensive suits with cowboy shirts and Stetsons when rumor had it he didn't really even enjoy ranching.

But he was a formidable businessman, smart and intimidating.

She had barely believed her luck when he'd promoted her to the vice president position. Of course, that arrogance of his made him so confident in his decisions that he'd missed the obvious these past months. Even when it was uncovered that Willem Inwood spread the rumors about Perry that threatened to tank stocks, no one had suspected her of playing a part.

It would almost be amusing how little they suspected her, if only her situation wasn't so dire, her goals finally so close she could almost taste success.

The catalyst for her grudge had come about so unexpectedly, in a quiet moment. She had been nostalgically going through her late dad's things in her attic when she discovered an old letter, from her father to her mother. He'd promised that he would change, that things would get better. She had been stunned to read that her father planned to ask the dying Harrington York for help. The man had promised him a tract of land on the outskirts of Houston that was reputed to be rich in oil.

Harrington York, whose daughter was married to none other than Sterling Perry.

Once a wealthy titan like Harrington and his son-in-law Sterling, her father drank and gambled and got himself into trouble, losing his fortune. But she'd known her dad wanted to reform and that land would have given him a second chance to do just that. But Angela's grandfather Harrington must have changed his mind because when he died that land went to Ryder Currin, who'd developed an oil empire from it. Currin, a nobody ranch hand rumored to be having an affair with Harrington's daughter, Tamara, Sterling's wife. Such pervasive gossip that Sterling's youngest offspring, Roarke, had submitted to a paternity test with Ryder Currin.

Negative.

But still.

Good Lord, these people were like an episode of a reality show. And she had paid the price for their selfishness.

Her mother had never reconciled with her dad, and her life fell apart. She'd lost everything because of Harrington's false promises, and the way the Currins and Perrys had greedily done what was best for them. Her temple throbbed at the thought of how fast her father had been forgotten. How fast her life had taken a downward spiral.

She had even, very reluctantly, given up her baby. She'd had no support system to help her raise her daughter, not like someone at this table would have had. Bitterness soured in her mouth, growing stronger every day.

Within a few years, her father drank himself to death, leaving behind a second wife and a son who she had refused to acknowledge as her brother.

Until this opportunity arose.

She didn't feel guilty about using him in her scheme. Why should she? He had a similar lack of conscience. Her brother was an easy mark because he'd always wanted the relationship with his sister that she'd denied him since birth. Her half brother had been more than eager to bring down the man "responsible" for destroying their father's future.

Her hands closed into fists under the table. There was still a chance her carefully laid plans could still unravel. Willem was in jail. Staying silent, sure. For now. Eventually the prosecutor would find the sweet-spot offer that would make Willem sing.

And then it would all be over. Job lost. Friends gone. Possible jail time for her, too, based on the roll of the dice. No amount of deep breaths could will away panic over the undeniable.

Because once they knew it was she—Tatiana Havery, Willem's half sister, Angela Perry's "best friend"—who'd orchestrated everything? Her time would have run out to make her enemies pay.

Esme was running low on patience. With herself, primarily.

She stood at the kitchen island, chopping a salad and wondering why and how she'd assumed control of entertaining matchmaking contestant number one—Amaryllis, the veterinarian, who was likely perfect for Jesse. Esme diced radishes faster and faster, struggling to appear unaffected by the brunette on the barstool.

Would she be the one Jesse chose for his perfect mate? She seemed right on the surface, given her career. Even Amaryllis's car was a better fit than Esme's destroyed Porsche.

The knife slipped, barely missing her thumb.

Jesse's dating life was not her business. It had no bearing on the situation with her father. She'd just shared a couple of kisses with Jesse Stevens, nothing more. Okay, so it had been, quite possibly, the best kiss of her life. All the more reason she should stay in her suite and work since he had plans to marry and propagate with a stranger.

But curiosity had her out here playing chef on the off chance of finding out why this woman was completely wrong for Jesse.

Radishes reduced to edible rubble, she moved on to cucumbers, still trying to study the woman without being obvious. The last thing she wanted was for Amaryllis to notice. Or worse yet, for Jesse to come back inside and catch her in an unguarded moment. He likely wouldn't be much longer talking to the ranch hands who'd made it back, thanks to their four-wheelers.

When Jesse had asked Amaryllis how she'd managed the drive in spite of the weather, she'd informed him she'd had lots of experience driving in all kinds of storms. After all, her work as a vet extended to farm animals. She'd navigated worse roads to assist in a delivery. Being punctual was important, she'd added, tapping her wristwatch. She had committed to being here at a certain time and she kept her commitments.

No spinning out in a sports car on a washed-out road for her, apparently.

Amaryllis sounded…too perfect.

Even from here, Amaryllis sat too straight. Like a rod shot through her back. Neatly trimmed nails painted a pale pink fiddled with her hair. The first bachelorette glanced down at her watch, then looked impatiently at the kitchen threshold.

Amaryllis broke any stereotypes Esme'd had about vets dressing in baggy scrubs even on their off days. A fitted lavender button-up shirt outlined her curves. Without so much as looking at Esme, the woman scrolled through her phone, pausing to type every so often. She delicately crossed her legs, clad in a pattern of thin black-and-gray pinstripes, as she ignored Esme's presence.

Esme skillfully scraped the chopped vegetables into a large pottery bowl before turning her attention to the grilled chicken breasts waiting to be sliced. "So what made you sign up for a matchmaker? If you don't mind my asking." The words came out of her mouth before her filter could catch them. Slicing the chicken breast into even strips, she waved her free hand. "Wait. Forget I said anything. It's none of my business."

Since walking into this house, she'd lost all damn control of herself. Frustration grew in her chest, and she continued the rhythmic slicing, attempting an air of casual sophistication and disinterest that Esme knew lingered somewhere inside her.

"I'm not ashamed at all. Ask away." Amaryllis pulled out a gold compact from her leather bag. Looking at herself in her reflection, the brunette fluffed her hair and then turned her attention to Esme. Unruffled and precise. "I'm a large-animal veterinarian, which means I spent almost every waking hour of my twenties studying. And now's not much better. I'm a workaholic who loves her job. There's not much chance for me to meet people who aren't affiliated with my practice."

Esme nodded, dumping the chicken into the bowl. Shifting her weight from left to right foot, she shrugged her shoulders, tension growing the longer the woman stayed.

"I would think that would actually give you plenty of opportunities to meet people who share interests with you. You didn't have to drive all the way out here to meet a rancher."

Was she trying to make Amaryllis leave?

Jesse wouldn't appreciate having his plans upset. And it wasn't that she actually had a problem with matchmakers. Plenty of her friends used dating websites, quite successfully. She'd even dipped her toes into those waters a couple of times.

She knew her questions were pushy and not even necessary, but she couldn't make herself stop.

Brows raising, Amaryllis pinned Esme with a matter-of-fact stare that threatened to shut down the conversation. "In my small town, the options are limited. This is the most efficient use of my time."

Amaryllis was too...practical for Jesse. Even though he proclaimed he was going this route for logical reasons, she could tell by his messy desk, it was all an act. He had a freer spirit than he wanted to admit.

"And you don't care that he has two other women coming?" The question sucked the air from the kitchen.

Amaryllis blinked fast, her lips going tight. Apparently, it did matter to her. And Esme felt bad for bringing it up. This really wasn't her business. But something like satisfaction clung to her regret for sharing Jesse's plans.

Which only made her feel worse. Confused her, too.

How did this happen? Esme felt the weight of why she was actually at Jesse Stevens's house crash on her shoulders. Her father's future as the president of the Texas Cattleman's Club. Not to scare away Jesse's suitors.

"I'm sorry," Esme said quickly, shoving aside

the bowl and racing to the other side of the island. "That wasn't my place. Talk to Jesse. He'll be back in a moment. I'll just get out of your way."

"I should be leaving." The lady vet moved faster toward the door, tugging her rain jacket on with each step.

Oh, hell. What had she done? She'd ruined everything. This wasn't going to help her father at all. She should have reined in her jealousy, damn it.

"He's a great guy." Esme fast-walked after her, her socked feet slippery against the tiled floor. "I can give you pointers on him, make up for the fact that I shouldn't have said anything."

Amaryllis turned quickly, her eyebrows shooting up in surprise. "So you're going to apologize for meddling by meddling some more?" With a bark of bitter laughter, she shook her head, securing her purse strap over her shoulder. Anger and embarrassment flared in the woman's brown irises. Looking her up and down with an X-ray stare, the woman pressed her lips together. "Wow, you're a piece of work."

Before Esme could think of a suitable response, the door was slamming. Esme tried to formulate a recovery plan. It was her forte, after all. But then she heard the sound of a car engine starting, tires crunching.

Any hope for salvaging the damage she'd caused extinguished as the engine sound faded.

Guilt pinched. Hard. She sagged back against the counter. She'd had no right to be jealous. But the feeling was still there all the same.

Why?

Did she have feelings for Jesse she was unwilling to explore? Yes, she was undeniably attracted to him. And they did have a lot in common, like having been brought up on a ranch. A strong work ethic. Humor.

But she certainly wasn't putting herself on the list of marriage candidates. She wasn't even sure she wanted to have children. Jesse hadn't hidden his plans for the future. In spite of her upbringing, she was a city girl, an executive who loved five-hundred-dollar shoes, in spite of the muck boots she'd worn earlier today.

That seemed like a lifetime ago.

The door opened again and Esme straightened. Had Amaryllis come back? No, the footfalls were too distinctly masculine.

Jesse stepped into the kitchen, sweeping off his Stetson. "Where's Amaryllis?"

Esme cleared her throat, knowing this could hurt her father's bid for a favor from Jesse, but unable to offer anything but the truth and a vow to herself that she would do better with the next two candidates. "I have a confession to make."

Six

A confession? Frowning, Jesse tossed his Stetson onto the kitchen island, keeping his eyes firmly on Esme's face and off the sight of her in jeggings and a long white button-down shirt.

Hey, wait, was that his?

He cleared his throat. "It's okay that you took my shirt."

She blinked uncomprehendingly for a moment. "Your shirt." She looked down and tugged the hem. "It was in the laundry. I hope you don't mind."

"No need to confess about riffling through my clothes. And with luck, your suitcase will be here tonight...or tomorrow." Would she be spending another night?

Not that it should matter. Not with his potential mates coming. Still, he selfishly craved more time.

Esme pursed her lips, her hand moving to the tall glass filled with ice and water. As she swirled the ice against the glass, he watched her grow more tense, her shoulders rising, her jaw clenching.

Her hand shook as she gripped her glass. "That's not my confession. You asked about Amaryllis. She's gone. As in left the property."

Tilting her head, she gestured to the now-empty driveway.

Running a hand through his hair, he tried to make sense of what she was telling him. Had he offended the lady vet somehow? "Where's she going? The Cozy Inn and the Cimarron Rose bed-and-breakfast are probably full with Christmas travelers."

Esme opened her mouth as if to speak, then clamped it shut. He took a step toward her, looking for some clarity.

"She's gone-gone. As in left town, not coming back." Esme crossed her arms over her chest defensively. "She wasn't right for you."

He frowned, surprised and confused. "When I went outside, she seemed quite eager to get to know each other better over dinner. What made her change her mind?" When she didn't answer right away, suspicion nipped at him. "Or should I ask *who* changed her mind? Esme?"

"That's my confession." She inhaled deeply, then blurted, "I let it slip that two other women are coming."

Even from here, he could see the whites of her fingertips as she gripped her water glass.

He rocked back on his boot heels. "That shouldn't have been a surprise to her, though. We both went through a matchmaker. Nothing's exclusive until we decide to date."

She couldn't help but think again how her mother had married her father because it was a practical match that pleased her family. Maybe that had something to do with why she and her siblings had stayed single for so long.

"How very…progressive of you." She nudged the salt grinder closer to the pepper mill.

"I take that to mean you're a romantic, all about the hearts and flowers and being swept off your feet."

"There's no need to make fun of me. I'm very sorry I chased off your new girlfriend. Oops. Not girlfriend. Your potential wife." She winced, resting her hand on his arm. "Wait, scratch that. I'm trying to apologize, not dig myself in deeper."

That small touch sent sensations zinging through him. Her eyes widened with that same awareness he felt, the undeniable attraction.

Then realization dawned. Esme was jealous of the women being sent by the matchmaker, had likely even chased Amaryllis off. That gave him more of a kick than it should, especially when she'd made it clear she wasn't looking for the same things as him in a relationship. Hadn't she?

"So if you don't want me seeing Amaryllis," he mused, heat flaring over his skin at her nearness, "does that mean you want to take that kiss further?"

Her lips worked silently for a moment, color rising in her cheeks. Her chest rose and fell faster, the curves of her breasts enticing. His hands itched to explore.

"You're egotistical." She stepped back. Away from him? Or away from temptation?

He wasn't going to let her off the hook that easily.

"And you like me." The realization was satisfying as hell.

"You're infuriating. And more importantly, you have two more women due here, when?" she asked with a challenge in her voice. She pointed to the window, at the cloudless sky.

"Tomorrow, most likely. The weather app on my phone showed that roads are starting to clear." Esme would be able to leave. "They were supposed to come today, but they texted while I was finishing up in the barn to say they're waiting, just to be safe."

Her jaw dropped. "You scheduled all three women today? At once?"

"I told you Amaryllis already knew about the others. She's a practical, down-to-earth woman."

He needed practical. Stable.

Esme's eyes fluttered closed, then opened again, sparking.

"Knowing about the other women is different than not caring. She had her hopes up, Jesse. You can mock romanticism all you want. It means something to some people, though. It clearly meant something to that woman who ran like hell from the prospect of being a party of some lineup of women for you to pick from."

"What if I were a part of a lineup of men for her?"

"I would find that sad, too," she said without hesitation.

"It doesn't seem like you approve of matchmakers."

She shook her head, her silken hair gliding over her shoulders. "You misunderstand. I have no problem with a matchmaker. I just think the way you're going about it is…"

"Is what?" he asked, more curious than he should be about how this woman's mind worked. "Spit it out."

"Fine." She braced her shoulders, her chin jutting. "I think it's a recipe for disaster. For heartache. Whatever you want to call it—romantic or practical—it just doesn't seem like something that will work long-term. Not that my opinion matters at all. It's your life."

Her criticism stung. He wanted a family of his own and put a lot of thought into how to approach this. And she just shot it all down in an instant as she stood in judgment of him. "You sure are being confrontational for a person who wants to persuade me your dad should lead that new chapter."

"I'm emotional. I can't make a spreadsheet of my feelings like you do." She grabbed her empty glass and stalked to the sink. "But no worries from here on out. I'll be sure the next two candidates hear only glowing things about you from me."

She stormed across the kitchen and toward the main part of the house without another word, anger crackling off her. His eyes were drawn to the sway of her hips as she walked away. Even after she was gone, her fragrance lingered.

As did his thoughts of what would have happened if Esme had been on that list.

Even two hours later, Esme couldn't believe what she'd said to Jesse. She was normally a calm professional. She was a middle-child peacemaker.

Not today, though.

She'd been hiding out here in her room since their argument, sitting in the middle of the bed and trying to make out a Christmas shopping list. A totally fruitless endeavor since her mind kept wandering back to their fight in the kitchen and how she'd wanted him to...

To what? She hugged the fat pillow, the high-thread-count cotton sensual against her skin.

Sighing, she had to admit the truth. She'd wanted Jesse to agree with her, then sweep her into his arms and kiss her until her knees melted.

The scent of something cooking, something fragrant and full of spices, teased her nose. She glanced at her clock and saw it was approaching suppertime. Would the time apart have hit the reset button for him as it had for her?

There was only one way to find out.

She tossed aside the pillow and slid off the bed, smoothing the shirt, his shirt that she'd pulled from the laundry. Her footfalls soft against the floor, she drew closer until she found Jesse standing at the dark stainless steel stove, stirring a pot of what looked like…

"Is that beef stew?" she asked, gripping and rubbing her wrist, a go-to gesture from when she had heated arguments with her sisters. A self-soothing gesture to calm herself. Not that Jesse knew that. But muscle memory was a powerful thing, and she needed all the smoothing-over vibes she could get.

He glanced back over his shoulder. "It is. Corn bread's in the oven."

"I would have thought you had staff to help you."

After all, he had a bunkhouse for ranch hands, and he'd mentioned a foreman. But his house was huge and quiet.

He continued stirring, pausing for a moment to smell the deep notes of pepper billowing off the steam. "I do, but they clean and leave. It's just me so they don't need to come often. And I cook for myself."

She stepped closer, dropping her grip on her wrist. "I'm sorry for what I said earlier. It's your life. You know what you want. And that's more than most people in the world."

"Thank you. Apology accepted."

"Does that mean I'm invited to supper?"

"I'm not going to starve you." He tasted the stew and her mouth watered. For him. "My mechanic said he'll get to your car in the morning for a better diagnostic. Unless you have family or friends you want to come get you now. If the rain gets much heavier, the roads could wash out even worse."

Leave? So soon? Apparently, he still was angry, and she couldn't blame him. "Are you asking me to go now? I'm not sure my family could get here safely. But I can still go. There must be lodging somewhere."

"No, that's not what I'm saying. Like I said before, I'm sure everything's booked anyway, given it's the Christmas season." His mouth kicked up into a smile. "And you're chasing women off my property who will need a place to stay since the rain picked up again."

He leaned to pull the corn bread out of the oven,

and she couldn't help but check out his butt. No female with a pulse would be able to deny how fine it was, denim cupping the perfect curve in a way that made her long to touch.

She squeezed her hands into fists on the kitchen island.

"Woman," she reminded him. "I've only chased off one woman."

He chuckled softly. "The week is young, Esme."

"It would help if you weren't so funny." Leaning against the cool granite countertop, she shook her head, taking in the subtle pull of his muscles as he stirred the stew.

"And it would help me if you weren't so sexy smart," he retorted.

"What does 'sexy smart' mean?"

He eyed her with a smoky gaze. "You have a brain that rivals your body. Smart women are sexy."

Her skin tingled with awareness. "Thank you for noticing…both. I worry because I work for my father that people may think I don't deserve the job. I try twice as hard to prove myself."

"Word around the club is that you're fierce at what you do. Have you ever thought about looking into switching companies?"

She'd thought of leaving—just once. But duty bound her to protect all that her father had built. Had sacrificed for. She couldn't walk away from the legacy.

"It's the family business. Plenty of relatives work together."

"Okay, fair enough." He leaned back. "So what do you say I dish up dinner and then you can tell me why your father is the best candidate to lead the new chapter of the Texas Cattleman's Club."

Surprise rippled through her. "Really? That simple? You're just asking me?"

"I am. I'll be looking into Ryder Currin. A few other possibilities, too."

"So my dad didn't need to send me here," she said softly.

"It shows how much he wants it. That means something. I get that he's excited about the new chapter. We all are." He passed her a bowl. "Now let's eat."

Companionably, they dished up their dinner, her mind scrolling through what she wanted to say.

Because yes, this club meant a lot to every one of them and she didn't want to say anything to mar the opening.

She could already envision the parties they would have there. The site had been chosen with care, a historic former luxury boutique hotel that fell into disrepair, now almost finished being renovated by Perry Construction. A gorgeous three-story building on a corner downtown. There were suites on the top floor for the president and chairman of the board. The second floor was for board members' and officers' offices and conference rooms. And the first floor contained the ballroom, a bar-style café club for members only, and the main meeting hall.

Stepping into Jesse's dining room, she stopped short at the sight of wineglasses and flickering candles. For a stew dinner?

It was incongruous and charming all at once. A smile lit her from the inside out.

More than just charming, actually. It was dreamy. This man had a romantic side, whether he wanted to admit it or not.

And she needed to remind herself that some other woman would be the recipient of that long-term. Possibly sooner rather than later, depending on what he thought of those next two candidates.

Resolved, she took her seat at the table to start her pitch on why her father was the person to lead the Houston chapter of the Texas Cattleman's Club.

The very last thing she wanted to be discussing with Jesse Stevens.

The next morning, Esme stared at the two newest matchmaking candidates who'd arrived bright and early, within minutes of each other, and were now getting a tour of the barn. The foreman had just pulled Jesse aside to point out some issue with one of the mares.

Esme was surprised Jesse had left her alone with the two new arrivals after how things went with

Amaryllis. He welcomed them and introduced her as a business associate in from Houston before he was called away.

Not that he'd gone far. She felt his gaze on her from across the barn. Warning her?

Biting her lip, she forced her attention back to her side of the stables. This go-round, she wouldn't let so much as a whisper of criticism pass her lips. Far from it, she intended to sing his praises. And to do so, she should learn a little more about them, to get a handle on the best way to help them impress Jesse.

So she flung herself into conversation with the two women in the barn, all the years of training to maneuver through intense situations coming into use now. Not that she could have ever imagined her professional training would prove handy while speaking to matchmaking candidates. But she handled Riley Jean Smith and Michelle Mendoza.

Esme turned her attention back to Riley Jean and remembered the woman mentioning something about having a six-year-old. "Where's your son?"

Riley Jean fluffed her long, wavy jet-black hair. "Staying with my mama. She loves special time with Lonnie Mac."

Esme pulled a smile. "That's what grandmothers are for."

Riley Jean scrunched her pixie-like face, blue eyes grave and serious. "She wants me to have time for myself. And honestly, even though the matchmaking company checks out the prospective dates carefully, I wanted to spend time with him on my own, to form my own opinion."

That made sense. Esme cocked her head to the side, as she petted one of the horses whose head poked out from the stall. The sorrel horse stretched beneath her hands, enjoying the attention.

Shaking her head, Riley Jean held up a hand. "Don't take that the wrong way. It's not like I think he's a serial killer or something. I researched him on the internet. You know, just the basics like his social media pages, his professional profile, college records, friends of his… You're single, too. You understand."

Riley Jean touched a hand to Esme's arm in what seemed like a strange act of camaraderie.

Staying on target was going to be a challenge. More than she had thought. With grit and determination, she willed words to her tongue. "Of course you should meet with him first. Sounds like your mother taught you to be a good mama."

"Thank you. I try."

Actually, the woman sounded a little stalkerish with all that checking up on him. Reasonable safety was one thing. Doing a deep dive into the internet was something else altogether.

Esme shifted her attention to the other woman. "So, tell me more about yourself."

Michelle leaned against the stall door—a vision

in heeled boots, jeans and a plaid shirt. Dark waves framed her tan face, making her brown eyes all the more striking. "I'm a former runner-up in the Miss Texas pageant, third runner-up."

"You're lovely. I'm surprised you didn't win."

"Me, too," she said with no indication that she grasped how egotistical that sounded. "I got thrown from a horse the week before the competition, hurt my hip, which made walking in heels a real bitch."

Michelle pushed herself off the stall door, offering her palm to the sorrel horse before petting it. From down the barn, the low timbre of Jesse's voice reverberated, though there was no telling what he was saying.

Esme resisted the urge to shout "fire" and send both women running. But she wasn't going to repeat her mistake by chasing them off. She owed her father—and Jesse—more than that. She needed to be better. She hated being ruled by jealousy whether it was about Jesse, her sisters or her dad.

If this was what Jesse wanted, then she would do her best to help make it happen.

Checking to make sure Jesse was still occupied with ranch business, Esme leaned closer to Riley Jean and Michelle. "I would like to help you both."

Michelle's microbladed eyebrows rose. "Both of us?"

Esme bit back a sigh. "This isn't *The Bachelor* where you're both trying to outdo the other."

Michelle rocked back and forth in her high-heeled boots with a chuckle. "Speak for yourself."

"Okay, that." Esme tapped Michelle on the arm. "He has a good sense of humor. He'll like that about you."

Michelle shook her hair back over her shoulders with a perfect toss. "I considered doing a stand-up comedy routine as my talent but opted for a patri-otic tap dance instead."

"Hmm… I'd say go with your first instinct from now on." Esme bit the inside of her cheek. "Riley Jean? I bet you miss your son."

"I do." She touched a heart locket around her neck. "He's the best thing that ever happened to me, and he's everything to me since my husband died. Do you want to see Lonnie Mac's picture?"

Riley Jean opened the locket to reveal a photo of a gap-toothed boy. A kid who would probably love to have Jesse's attention.

"Cute kid," Esme said, in spite of herself. "Hav-ing a family is very important to Jesse. He really wants kids."

A reminder she needed to take to heart.

"Whoa, hold on," Riley Jean protested. "That's getting ahead of things. I only just showed up."

Esme felt the crisis boiling and knew she had to do her best to douse it. "I just meant it's okay to talk about your son. I've seen single-mom friends of mine hold back sharing about their kids for fear it'll chase the guy away. That's not the case here."

Riley Jean smiled impishly. "That's all good to know. Thank you."

Esme fidgeted with the ends of her sleeves, ready for this to be over but knowing there was still a task in front of her. "PR is my chosen profession. It's all about taking the facts and putting the right spin on things."

Michelle looked her up and down. A moment passed before she opened up her bubble gum–pink lips. "I have one last question."

Esme nodded. "Sure. Shoot."

"Why aren't you going after Jesse when you clearly know—and admire—so much about him?"

Surprise slammed into her. A fair question. She looked down the barn to where he worked with a horse. He was so handsome, even covered in dirt, his muscles apparent as he gripped the horse's hoof for more treatment for the abscess.

He was earthy, handsome and, yes, "sexy smart."

As if Jesse sensed her looking at him, he glanced over at her. His green eyes glinted and he smiled. She smiled back. How could she not?

Michelle's sigh and a creak of leather across the room drew Esme's attention back. Riley Jean was gathering her purse and Michelle was tugging on her jacket.

Oh, damn.

Esme straightened quickly and double-timed after them, barely catching them at the barn door. "Where are you going? Did I say something wrong?"

Michelle tucked her head to the side with a half smile. "Honey, you didn't have to say a word. Your body language said it all. You've got it bad for that man."

Riley Jean nodded. "And by the steamy look he just smoked your way, he has it bad for you, too."

Did he?

She looked over at him quickly, and uh-oh, he was already striding toward her, no doubt because of the rapidly departing women. How had they gotten so far ahead of her already? Panic nipped at her as she called out, "Wait."

But Michelle and Riley Jean were deep in conversation as they moved toward their vehicles, heads tilted together.

"What's going on?" Jesse asked as he closed the distance between them.

Esme met him at the open barn door, chilly air from outside blasting through. "I swear I didn't do a thing to chase them off. In fact, I told them great things about you."

He turned from the door back to her, steam— the sensual kind—smoking from him in palpable waves. "Like what?"

She couldn't believe her ears. She gave him her

full attention as the women drove off. Her pulse picked up speed. "You're not angry over them leaving?"

He planted a hand on the doorframe beside her. "Surprisingly, no. Not at all." He stroked back a strand of her hair, drawing two fingers down the lock. "My focus is exactly where it should be."

Butterflies churned in her stomach and she realized, truly realized and acknowledged for the first time, that there was something between them that just couldn't be ignored. Breathless and dry-mouthed, she couldn't deny that she wanted him.

Before she could have second thoughts that could rob her of exploring those feelings, she said, "That's really convenient."

He worked that lock of her hair around his finger, slowly drawing her closer. "How so?"

"Because," she blurted, the words tumbling out of her mouth faster than she intended, "I was thinking perhaps I could try out to be one of your dates."

Seven

Jesse stared at Esme in shock.

Surely he couldn't have heard her correctly. Although the surge of passion shooting through him shouted how much he hoped he had. He wasn't even disappointed to see the three supposedly perfect candidates bail. His thoughts were too wrapped up in Esme.

"Try out?" he asked, pulling the barn door closed, sealing them back inside, a few stray pieces of hay crunching under his boots. "What exactly do you mean by that? Audition to be my wife?"

"That might be a bit of a quick leap down the aisle. But a test run as your girlfriend—your wife, if you will—could give me the chance to see if I really like it." She shifted in her boots. Her blond hair fell over her blouse, hinting at her curves.

"You're certain of what you're suggesting? After everything you said about the matchmaking process?" His brow raised as he leaned against the stall door. Duke poked his head out of the stall, tilting it sideways. The horse chuffed, knocking his muzzle into Jesse.

A wide grin broke across Esme's face, lighting her eyes. She reached up to ruffle Duke's forelock.

"Part of me feels like that's all I want for Christmas," she said earnestly, her blue eyes sparkling. "To be honest, the other part of me isn't sure about anything, particularly life on a ranch and one that's not even near my relatives."

He liked that family was important to her. How ironic that until now he hadn't thought of that being a core part of who she was. So much so that she'd risked her life coming out here in a horrible storm just because her father had asked for her help. He started to churn over the possibility of chucking the matchmaker notion and giving an earnest shot at seeing where the attraction to Esme led.

"And you're okay with this, even though we barely know each other?"

"Seriously? You're asking me that?" She snorted on a laugh. "You were willing to consider marrying someone you'd never even met in person."

"Fair statement." He cupped her shoulders, then slid his hands down her arms, linking fingers.

"Although now that I think about it, your matchmaker had you fill out a profile. So let's do that."

"You want to take a survey now?"

"Not a written one. We can do it verbally." She leaned closer, the heat of her breath a tempting caress. "Organically."

"Hmm, sounds intriguing. Do you want to go back to the house or to the office?"

She inclined her head, voice husky. "Your office. It's closer."

His heart rate picked up the pace. "After you, ma'am."

He gestured toward his office, following her inside. The Christmas tree lit the room well enough, so he didn't turn on the overhead light.

Esme settled onto the leather sofa, leaving space for him. "I'll start easy. What's your favorite music?"

"Country, acoustic." He sat beside her, stretching his arms along the back of the couch, his fingers brushing against her. "Simple but rich."

"Mmm, sexy answer. I can imagine long, slow kisses with guitar music in the background." Her eyes flamed, lighting an answering fire in him. "I like soft rock, old classics. And there's common ground there to be found in coffeehouse styles of the tunes."

"Favorite author?"

Esme tapped her fingers along a stack of magazines on the table beside the couch. "Jane Austen. Favorite movie?"

"*True Grit*, the original. All Stetsons, all the time." Watching Westerns was a ritual he'd started with his grandfather long ago. Funny how he hadn't thought about that until now.

"What's an absolute no-no in a relationship?"

Her question surprised him, but his answer was easy and earnest. "Lying."

A pained wince twitched at her face. Lines of worry etched her brow. It made him wonder what had happened in her past to cause them. And made him want to ensure it would never happen again.

She braced her shoulders. "Agreed."

Good. "If you could live anywhere other than Texas, where would it be?"

"There is nowhere other than Texas." Tucking her feet beneath her, she preened like a cat.

He threw back his head and laughed, full-out. He liked the way she could draw that from him. "Ah, perfect answer. Your turn."

Esme pursed her lips. "When was the last time you cried?" Then she shook her head. "Never mind. I don't really expect you to respond to that. Male machismo being what it is."

She might say it didn't matter, but she must have asked for a reason. He'd already gleaned that her father was a controlling type. Certainly, Sterling Perry had a reputation of being all business, all flash. No substance?

Had that question been a Freudian slip? Was Esme looking for more from the people in her life?

Regardless, he had no problem offering her an honest answer. He looked past his desk to a nondescript piece of tack on the wall. "The day my horse Apollo died. I'd had him since I was a kid. I still keep his leather halter hanging there." He pointed to the wall. "I won't be putting it on another horse."

"I'm so sorry for that loss. It sounds like Apollo was an amazing friend to you."

Apollo had gotten him through every tough time in high school. He'd left it all behind when he rode. "I told you my family wasn't close. That led me to spend most of my time in the stables. Everyone there brought me up, taught me a good work ethic, taught me about life."

"You're truly tugging at my heart here."

He traced a finger along her cheekbone, just under her eye. "When was the last time you cried?"

"When my shoe broke in the rain." She angled to nip his finger.

He chuckled, his hand cupping her shoulder and drawing her closer. "Have you considered designer boots? I bet you would rock them."

She flattened her hands on his chest, her palms

warm. "Well, thank you for the lovely compliment, cowboy."

"I think we're finding we have more in common here than we expected." Her scent tempted him, enticed him, sending blood surging south.

"And we didn't even need the matchmaker." She stroked sensual circles on his chest that seared through his flannel shirt.

"And you do realize a part of being a wife means being in my bed?"

Her hands slid up his chest to loop around his neck. "That's the part I'm most looking forward to."

Esme didn't consider herself an impulsive person, but she'd never been more certain of anything. She wanted to make love to Jesse Stevens. Here, now, in this office that felt so much more like the essence of him than his perfectly decorated home he'd put together with a laser focus on creating some mythical family.

Reality was better than dreams.

Reality with *this* man.

She met him halfway for the kiss, not that far to move as they were both already angling forward. The hot sweep of his tongue along hers was bold and hungry. His spicy scent filled her every breath. Everything about the moment seared into her senses in a way she knew she would replay in memory again and again.

His fingers speared through her hair, massaging along her scalp as he drew her head closer. She sank deeper into the kiss and delicious sensations licked along her spine. She glided her fingers down his back and tugged the tails of his shirt from the waist of his jeans, tunneling up to stroke the muscled expanse of his back.

A frenzy burned at her even as she ached to savor every touch, taste, caress. Drawing the moment out sharpened the edge of desire, dulled the edge of time until she whispered against his mouth, "I'm ready to show you my sexy brain."

He chuckled, his hands gliding down to clasp her hips. "Oh really?"

"Yes, and more."

He growled softly in appreciation. "I'm looking forward to it."

"You'll reciprocate, of course."

He angled back to meet her gaze. "Am I moving too fast for you?"

She struggled to gather her thoughts and how to express herself when she still had so many questions herself. "To be honest, I've never felt this much for someone so quickly. So yes, my head is spinning more than a little, but I'm sure. Very sure that this is what I want."

"For what it's worth," he said, "even with the whole matchmaker gig, this is moving at lightning speed for me, too."

"But you're sure?" she repeated.

"Absolutely. I want you. Here. Now."

"All I needed to hear."

As soon as she said the words, he slid from the couch to kneel in front of her, the lit tree glimmering behind him.

Between kisses, he eased her sweater over her head, breaking briefly to tug it off and toss it aside. The air was cool against her flesh, then warm as he touched her again, unhooking her bra, freeing her for his touch and gaze. He peeled down her jeggings, his hands warm, launching butterflies in her stomach and goose bumps along her skin.

He reclined her back onto the sofa, his lips grazing her neck, nuzzling aside her sweater to nip along her collarbone. He was definitely overdressed, and she intended to fix that. Immediately. She made quick work of the buttons on his shirt, shoving the flannel off his broad shoulders, flinging it aside. Then... Wow... Just wow... His chest was on display, a feast for her eyes and hands. She arched up for another kiss, desire pulsing through her, demanding more. Of this moment. Of him.

She tucked her hands into his jeans pocket and whispered against his mouth. "Birth control?"

"Yes, I have it."

"So glad." She teased his bottom lip between her teeth.

"Me, too." He rested his forehead against hers for a moment before rolling to his feet.

He fished out his wallet, withdrew a condom and set it on the coffee table on top of a stack of farming magazines.

She swung her legs off the sofa and reached for him, unfastening his jeans. Easing the zipper down. Revealing the steely length of him. She stroked up, then down again. His hands gripped her shoulders, his chest rising and falling faster until he kicked aside his jeans and boxers. He angled back down to join her, stretching out over her in a delicious weight, his bare body meeting hers. She passed him the condom and quickly, he was ready.

And she was more than ready.

His gaze held hers as he slid inside her, filling her in a slow, deliberate stroke. Holding. The sensation of being connected for the first time was so intense, a ripple shimmered through her. Then he moved, and she moved with him, instinct taking over.

His mouth grazed her ear, her neck, before settling, yes, on her breast. Need tightened through her, sending her arching up. Her nails scored down his back lightly, although it was a struggle not to dig her fingers in deeply, anchor them both even more firmly.

She drew her foot up his calf and a husky moan rumbled in his chest. She'd known the attraction between them was strong, but she still hadn't expected the chemistry to be this intense, more than she'd felt with anyone before. Soon, too soon, she felt release building. And as much as she wanted to hold back, to wait, the bliss increased, growing more intense until her head was flung back with the force of her orgasm. Feeling Jesse's hoarse groans of completion heat her skin sent aftershocks along her already-sensitive nerves. Every sense was heightened, honed to right now.

His head was buried in her neck, his breath ragged, until with a hefty exhale, he rolled to his side, taking her with him. He eased a hand away to pull a blanket from the back of the sofa and over them, holding her close, staying silent other than the sound of their hearts galloping in sync.

As she drifted off to sleep, her walls and defenses down, she couldn't escape the niggling voice telling her that this had been a dangerous idea.

And already she wanted him again.

Their interview that afternoon had gone beyond anything he'd imagined. He could certainly check "sexually compatible" off his list. Their lovemaking still lingered in his mind. He already craved her again.

Jesse paced in the sunroom off his bedroom suite, glass walls overlooking his property. In the landscape lights the pool glimmered, spa waters churning. The bunkhouse glowed in the distance. Christmas lights glinted along the split-rail fences, marking the lines of his property out in the distance.

Space, waiting to be filled.

For a moment, he allowed himself to envision what the future might look like. And what it might look like with Esme in it. He dropped into one of the wingbacks, a glass of whiskey in his hand. His memory was full of images of her asleep in his bed, hugging a pillow, her honey-blond hair fanned around her. He wanted to make the most of his time with her, and it would be helpful to know how much time he had before he would have to make some trips up to Houston. It would help to find out about the state of the roads.

Checking the time, he found it just shy of midnight. He didn't want to wake anyone up…but then, his friend was a night owl. He typed out a text to his friend Nathan Battle, the sheriff of Royal.

Are you awake? If not, I'll catch up in the morning.

Seconds after he hit Send, the phone rang, Nathan's number flashing.

Jesse answered. "Thanks for calling. Hope I'm not disturbing you."

"Everyone's asleep or playing video games. What can I do for you?" Nathan was an imposing leader for their police force, with a soft spot for his wife, Amanda, and their children.

Jesse moved out onto the balcony. A few stars peeked out of the nighttime clouds. "How're the roads looking?"

"We have a couple of rural routes that are washed out and a damaged bridge. But we've marked enough detours for people to get around."

"I imagine you've had your hands full."

"Amanda's been on me to take a vacation once this is over." Nathan's wife owned the Royal Diner, an informal eatery where small-town Texas gossip got spread.

"Sounds like you're married to a wise woman." Nathan and Amanda had the kind of rock-solid marriage that was an advertisement for matrimony.

"I'm a lucky bastard," his gravelly voice echoed over the phone line. "But you didn't call me for a weather report. If you wanted to know about the state of the roads you could have phoned anyone in the department."

"What do you think of all the jockeying for power going on over in Houston to decide who's going to head the new club?" Of all his friends, Nathan was like a brother to Jesse. He'd served as sound counsel for years.

"I think we've been lucky to have our group stay local here for a long time. We've got a good town here and the club has made great strides since admitting women. The Texas Cattleman's Club stands for community and family, honor and friendship, a cohesive force to support each other and do good in the community."

Though his friend couldn't see, he still found himself nodding in agreement. For all those reasons he took his role in the Texas Cattleman's Club seriously. "I agree."

"Choosing the person to set the tone in Houston is important. We don't want our brand to be turned into some kind of social club or to lose its values. Houston isn't Royal. It's going to take a strong leader to guide all those larger-than-life personalities."

"Solid insights." His throat tightened. He hesitated.

A yawn echoed from the other end of the phone. "Do you mind if I ask why we're discussing this?"

Shooting a glance at his bed and finding Esme stirring just a bit, he moved farther out onto the balcony and kept his voice low. "I've got an unexpected guest here. Sterling Perry's daughter. She's come to town to lobby for her father."

"What do you think?"

He blinked. How in the hell did he answer that? "What do I think of *her*? Esme's brilliant."

"Uh-huh." Nathan chuckled.

"Uh-huh what?"

Nathan laughed softly again. "My friend, I've

been in this job a very long time and that's taught me how to read a person's tone. The sound always tells more than the words. And your tone tells me you are head over ass infatuated with her."

"And if I am? But she's the epitome of Houston glamour." Opposite of everything he thought he wanted during the whole matchmaking process. And yet he couldn't help but feel drawn to her.

"Glamour isn't a bad thing. You've been to enough galas at the club—tuxedos and gowns and jewels. I defy you to find any event more high-end than ours."

"Good point. Esme would enjoy that." He envisioned her in a floor-length ball gown. Dancing. Their bodies in sync as they moved to the music.

"And since you contacted that matchmaker, I assume your interest is still for something lasting. A wife and family?"

"My plans haven't changed."

"Then my advice? Pursue her. Find out if what you're feeling for her is the real thing."

Before Nathan had even finished signing off, Jesse's mind was already churning with ideas and excitement.

Dinner out. Maybe they could even double-date with his neighbor Cord and his girlfriend, Zoe. Cord would be relocating to Houston soon and Jesse was going to miss him. But then, connections in Houston would also give him a reason to see Esme.

Houston might have massive department stores, but Royal offered top-notch specialty niche shops, and he wouldn't mind having Esme along as he finished his Christmas shopping. And he still had a tree to chop down for all those decorations and an old-school string of lights like he remembered from childhood.

Full of plans, he pushed to his feet. He intended to show her just how amazing life could be here. That the town of Royal had everything to offer for a full social calendar.

And he very much looked forward to wooing her all the way back to his bed.

Eight

The past two weeks had been a blur of bliss for Esme, a time of discovery, getting to know Jesse, their differences fading in the face of so many shared interests, laughs and kisses. They'd spent nearly every moment together, going on dates, buying last-minute Christmas gifts and adding to the scant wardrobe in her suitcase. Touring his land, decorating his Christmas tree, making love in front of the fire.

He'd learned she had a weakness for flowers and could eat her way to the bottom of a bowl of popcorn. Heavily buttered. She sang Christmas carols with gusto, her pitch questionable, her enthusiasm undeniable.

Her equestrian skills were some of the best he'd ever seen. She was fire in motion on a horse.

Esme was a sensual woman who took pleasure in experiencing life.

Their nights had been spent passionately exploring in a lengthy quest to discover what made the other unravel with desire.

But she knew their time together was drawing to a close. She would have to return to Houston and her job. She'd delayed as long as she could.

Tomorrow, she was due to go back to Houston. Key members of the Royal chapter—including Jesse—would be touring the new club's building renovations. Afterward, there would be a meeting with those Royal players, held at the Houston site.

Cases would be made for who should be the new president. Had she done enough good during her time here? Heaven knew, she'd been focused more on her relationship with Jesse than on her father's bid for power.

She shoved aside the pinch of guilt. There was nothing she could do about that now, and she wouldn't let it steal the joy of this last evening with Jesse.

Tonight, they were enjoying a five-star dinner at the Texas Cattleman's Club—the original branch—

in Royal. Music from a string quartet filled the room with classical Christmas melodies.

Looking around, no one would guess the place had suffered a devastating tornado, the fiercest to hit Royal in nearly eighty years. They'd rebuilt, better than ever. Pride surged in her heart at this community, the bonds made in this space. No wonder Jesse felt like these people were family. His comfort here showed in his easy manner, his way of greeting friends who stopped by their table.

The club was housed in a large, rambling single-story building made of dark stone and wood. The interior decor consisted of mostly dark wood floors, leather upholstered furniture and super-high ceilings.

Hunting trophies and historical artifacts adorned the paneled walls. Her favorite was the tooth of an ancient relative of a horse. As a child, she'd been delighted to know herds of horselike creatures roamed the lands she called home. She'd even had her own horse tooth in a small shadow box that always felt strangely comforting to her. That the Royal club boasted a similar horse tooth gave a sense of continuity between the two spaces. A slice of home for her. In addition to the elegant formal dining hall, there were several private meeting rooms and a great room for both public and private Texas Cattleman's Club events.

During her tour of the place prior to being seated

for dinner, she'd been most surprised to discover the club had a childcare center for club members and employees, the laughter and squeals broadcasting how much the kids enjoyed the setup.

To see how inclusive the Texas Cattleman's Club had become warmed her even on the somewhat chilly Texas evening.

And of course, that was just the inside. Outdoors there was a stable, a pool, tennis courts and even a playground. Her mind was spinning.

She pulled her attention back to the table, tapered candles flickering in the middle of an arrangement of white poinsettias and holly.

She spooned up the last of her chocolate trifle. "Thank you, Jesse. This is the perfect end to an incredible meal, from the lobster bisque to the filet mignon."

"I'm glad you enjoyed yourself." He stretched a leg out. He'd worn his good boots with the suit.

"This has been an amazing two weeks."

He clasped her hand across the table. "I agree. I don't want things to end just because we're going to Houston."

Her chest grew tight. It was ironic how excitement and anxiety could make such a tangle. "I feel the same." Not wanting to risk wrecking their evening by wading into deep waters too soon, she said, "I'm looking forward to you meeting my family."

"I'm sure they'll be glad to have you back," he said with a pensive look in his green eyes.

She reached for her wine, avoiding his gaze, not ready to have the Houston-versus-Royal discussion yet. She sipped the after-dinner wine, then set the crystal glass on the table again. Her fingers tapped nervously along the gold beading at the glass stem, syncing with the Christmas carol playing softly.

The silence between her and Jesse stretched until she looked up self-consciously, pulling her hand away from the glass and clenching her fingers. She nodded toward the string quartet. "'Silent Night.' It was my mother's favorite carol."

"You must miss her a lot this time of year."

"Very much." She blinked back tears. "We all do. Even my dad, although their marriage wasn't the best. She married him out of duty. He married her for power. It's no surprise things didn't work out well at all."

"Is that why you reacted so strongly to the matchmaker idea?" he asked insightfully.

She could only nod, not trusting her voice.

He clasped her hand again. "Thank you for telling me that."

"Thank you for listening." She swallowed down a lump in her throat, then drew in a shaky breath. "Okay, that's enough serious talk for one night. I just want to enjoy this night of Royal's finest. In fact, I'm thinking we should order more dessert to take home and enjoy later."

"That sounds like an excellent idea. How about you choose for the both of us and surprise me?" Jesse placed his linen napkin by his plate. "And while you're doing that, I need to have a quick word with my friend Cord. I won't be long."

"Take your time." She smiled, soaking up the sight of him in a charcoal-gray suit and festive red tie.

"You really are incredible." Jesse's gaze smoked over her from across the table, lingering on the plunging neckline of the emerald velvet dress she'd chosen in one of the specialty boutiques at the Courtyard Shops. He dropped a kiss on her lips before stepping away.

Her toes curled in her Valentino heels. Tingles spread through her all the way down to her fresh pedicure.

The day had been deliciously pampering from start to finish. While Jesse had had business to attend to at his lawyer's, he'd suggested she spend the day at Royal's Saint Tropez Salon. She hadn't expected such a luxurious, high-end spa in a small town. She'd felt petty for judging so quickly.

Her appointment at the salon had afforded her time for reflection. Something about lavender-scented towels and rubs peeled away stress. And

the relative silence had helped. It had forced con-
templation. Forced reflection.

Truth be told, these weeks with Jesse had domi-
nated that reflection. How wrong she'd been about
him. The silly but serendipitous circumstances of
their meeting. How lucky they'd both been to find
each other because of the chaos of the storm. Ironic,
she'd mused, for a man who craved stability and
practicality.

She'd met so many incredible people over the
past couple of weeks, some of whom were seated in
the dining room tonight. She smiled in response to
Megan and Whit Daltry. Megan ran the local animal
rescue, Safe Haven. Jesse had brought Esme along
when he'd dropped off a donation to help with the
rescue's three horses recently taken in. Esme had
been amazed at the large operation, one that was
apparently growing exponentially under Megan's
leadership.

Megan and Whit were dining with Natalie and
Max St. Cloud, a fascinating couple. Even though
Max was a tech genius billionaire, his wife still
owned and operated the Cimarron Rose bed-and-
breakfast, with a small bridal dress shop attached.
Both couples' children were enjoying a Christmas-
themed movie night in the childcare center.

Her heart tugged at the memory of glimpsing
those sweet little faces when Jesse had taken a de-
tour there to pass out Christmas candy. They all

clearly knew and adored him. And she couldn't deny being enticed by the notion of a baby of her own someday, and celebrating family Christmases.

A cleared throat pulled her attention back. She found Zoe Warren, Cord's girlfriend, standing by the table. The towering brunette looked stunning in a simple gold sheath dress. Esme had enjoyed getting to know her and Cord during a lunch at the Royal Diner.

Zoe smiled genuinely. Drink in hand, she gestured to the table. "I hope I'm not interrupting your dinner."

"Not at all. I'm glad you came over." Esme stood quickly and then greeted her with a welcoming hug. "Have a seat. It looks like our dates are deep in a conversation that isn't close to wrapping up."

"Thank you. I would like that." Zoe settled into a chair beside her. "I enjoyed our lunch the other day."

A phantom gurgle tickled her stomach, even though she was far from hungry. Lunch with Zoe the other day had been at a small, vaguely yellowing local spot. Esme had her doubts as she crossed through the metal door. But after sitting down, her senses had been delighted. She felt as if she'd stumbled upon a contender for one of those reality television shows about stellar restaurants with questionable exteriors.

And the diner's food—she'd ordered the chicken-fried steak and a glass of sweet tea—had been every bit as wonderful as the interior. "The Royal Diner is one of those fun finds off the beaten path of major cities."

Zoe sipped her champagne, bubbles climbing up the crystal flute. "It's incredible how Amanda and Nathan Battle juggle two such busy careers with family life. I've lost count of how many children they have."

Esme toyed with the stem of her wineglass pensively. "It sounds like they have it all."

"That they do." Zoe grinned, motioning to the waiter who was walking by with a tray of champagne. She took another flute before looking back at Esme. "So how are you liking the rest of Royal?"

"Surprisingly very much. It's not Houston, of course," Esme said with a shrug, unworried about judgment since the woman was from Houston, as well, "but I've found there's much more offered here than I expected. It's a unique mix of a small town with some big-city amenities."

"It's quite a haven." Zoe glanced over at her handsome dark-haired boyfriend, concern furrowing her forehead. "I worry he's going to miss Royal and all his friends here. But he insists he's committed to making a move to Houston for me. He's bought the loveliest ranch on the outskirts of town. He's making such a big sacrifice for me. For us."

Zoe was a police detective in Houston. Her investigation into Vincent Hamm's murder had brought her here to Royal. Esme and her family owed Zoe a debt of gratitude, the cop's progress going a long way to help shift the cloud of suspicion off Sterling Perry.

Esme toyed with the placement of her silver dessert spoon. "How incredible that he's willing to move for you."

"We're in love." She looked toward her boyfriend, her face full of emotion. "We found a compromise, because the option of being apart was more than we could bear."

Esme's gaze skated to Jesse deep in conversation with his friend and she wondered...

If Cord was willing to relocate to Houston, might Jesse be willing to make the move, as well? Tomorrow would be pivotal for more than her father.

Her own future with Jesse rode on their trip to Houston.

Ryder Currin paced through the Houston building of the Texas Cattleman's Club, checking last-minute touches to the structure's renovations before the contingent from Royal arrived tomorrow. Angela walked alongside him, making her own notes in her tablet, the scent of paint heavy in the air. He could hardly believe the plans for starting this Houston branch were coming to fruition. Ryder had been instrumental in bringing the chapter to Houston, and yes, he craved the position as president.

He wanted to lead the organization through this transitional time.

But would that ambition threaten his second chance with Angela, given how much her father wanted the same thing?

Telling himself it was pointless to borrow trouble, he pulled his attention back to the building, his boot steps echoing up to the soaring ceiling.

The location and architectural style for the Houston chapter's future home was very different from the Royal club. It had seemed an insurmountable project at first, since the historic former luxury boutique hotel had fallen into disrepair. But all their plans for renovation were coming together, thanks to Perry Construction. The three-story edifice had always been stunning on the outside. Now the inside matched.

The location was practical for so many reasons, including the fact that three doors down was the Houston Galleria Hotel, a medium-sized luxury hotel where members could stay when in town.

Angela's high heels clicked on the floor as she walked ahead of him, caught up in her notes. This club was important to her, too. Ryder understood she was caught in a tough position with both him and her father wanting the lead position here. He didn't want anything to interfere with this second chance they had. He would withdraw if it came to that, but she'd insisted this should play out as the club decided.

He just wanted to make sure there was no negative blowback as they rolled out the official grand opening with a New Year's Eve bash. Press releases for the event had been delayed with Esme Perry out of town for so long.

They'd all been thrown for a loop when Angela's sister had decided to stay in Royal even after the storm passed. And of course, Sterling had been all too willing to accommodate time off work so his daughter could spend more time currying family favor.

Ryder was a man who abided by the rules, so this flagrant lobbying really chapped his hide. It just wasn't fair play.

Angela made everything more complicated. He loved her. Deeply. Truly. In a way that made his soul sing, something he hadn't expected to happen again after his wife Elinah had died. He didn't underestimate how important it was to get this right with Angela. His first marriage had ended in divorce. He couldn't regret the union since his son, Xander, had come from that relationship. But his breakup with Penny was still a failure that marked him.

One he wouldn't allow himself to repeat.

The rumors that he'd had feelings for Angela's mom were true. But he'd never acted on those feelings because of respect for rules and fair play. Honor

meant something to him. Besides, his second marriage had shown him what real love was. Elinah. A
part of his heart would always belong to her. Their
time together had been the best, years that gave
him his daughter Annabel and then they'd adopted
Maya. Losing Elinah to cancer had almost destroyed
him.

He wouldn't go through that heartbreak again. He
would do whatever it took to keep he and Angela's
love safe. There'd be no repeat of their breakup. Already he could envision her living in his home. His
log-style mansion wasn't as fancy as the Perry place.
He'd grown up poor and had never been comfortable with ostentation.

Still, the place had been plenty roomy to bring
up his children with space to spare. And for more
children?

Ryder looked at Angela. He saw the weight that
seemed to press down on her, to change her normal happy expression. He hated to see her sad. "I'm
sorry your sister missed the brunch she had planned
with you, Melinda, Tatiana and my girls."

He was, truly, although secretly he was always
antsy when Angela or his daughter Maya spent
time with Tatiana. The woman was a shark with
the power to upset their lives.

"The brunch will still happen, I'm sure." A brief
flash of disappointment flickered in Angela's eyes
before she schooled her features. "We haven't set a

specific date. Just sometime whenever Esme gets back."

She noticed a paint droplet on a nearby marble plant stand and Ryder watched her as she worked to eradicate it.

"Well, keep me in the loop." A glint caught his eyes. Stooping down, he picked up a stray nail from beneath a windowsill and pocketed it. Still so much to do.

"About my sister's return?"

Shrugging, he ran a hand through his hair and then stopped at the nape of his neck. "Sure, and the brunch."

Muffled noises grabbed his attention. Shouting and angry voices. He locked eyes with Angela. Her brow furrowed in confusion.

His daughter Maya shouldered past the painters putting last-minute touches on some trim. She raced toward him in a flurry of color with her bold yellow coat and her vibrant red hair. His youngest child had never been one to get lost in the shuffle of day-to-day life.

"Dad, I have to talk to you," she demanded, her raised voice echoing upward as she crashed into the room. Panting and distraught, she wasn't budging.

"Well, hello to you, too, Maya. It's good to see you. Angela and I are almost through here—"

"No, Dad. Not later. Now. There are so many rumors flying around about our family, too many secrets. I can't—I won't—wait any longer. I'm eighteen. It's time we finally had this talk." She stomped her foot in exasperation, but her eyes were filled with tears.

Regret hit him in the chest, that he'd brought his daughter to this level of anxiety.

Angela clasped his arm, a welcome touch when Maya's outburst had him reeling. "I've got plenty to occupy me. Please, take as long as you need."

She gave his arm a final squeeze before walking off toward a pile of plaster dust beneath a gilded mirror, snapping photos with her tablet.

"Thank you," he said, appreciating that she understood and accepted how important his children were to him. He tucked an arm around his daughter's shoulders and guided her to the café area free of painters.

Maya gasped for air beside him, her shoulders shaking in a way that telegraphed how close she was to losing it. He'd put enough bandages over skinned knees and listened to enough of her high school drama to read the signs.

He guided her to a club chair and dropped into another one across from her. "What's going on, Maya? These rumors about the family business have been circulating for a while now. What made today so upsetting?"

Maya closed her eyes tightly. Took a deep breath. Then another.

Ryder could see her mouth moving as she counted to ten before she opened her eyes. His fire-haired child had always struggled to rein in her emotions.

"It's been building up for a long time, and then when the invitations went out for the mother-daughter tea today..." She picked at the wrist of her yellow coat. "I need you to tell me the truth, once and for all."

A sigh all but deflated him. Hearing about the mother-daughter tea sucker punched him, even after all these years since Elinah died. He would always miss her. She'd been a loving wife and mother. He'd tried to make up for what his children had lost... but it was an impossible void to fill.

Then a dark thought hit him. Maya was asking about her biological mother. He'd promised to tell her when she was eighteen and he'd put it off long enough. The pit in his gut grew deeper.

"The truth?" he asked, stalling to give himself time to collect his thoughts for a conversation that would undoubtedly prove difficult. Those secrets had been a heavy weight on the shoulders of a man who prided himself on honesty and honor.

"About my biological parents." Her eyes were clear, her tone steely. "No more delaying. Tell me now, or I'm never going to talk to you again."

There was no missing the vehemence in her voice. Her arms crossed tightly over her chest in a protective hug as she bit down on her lip. Ryder could feel fear and anger radiate from her in waves.

She'd asked in the past, but never pushed. They'd done a kind of dance with the subject, her pressing, then backing away as if she was afraid of the truth.

And there was reason to be wary, the same reason he'd held back telling her until she was old enough to handle the truth. But she was eighteen now, no denying that.

He took her hands in his and thought back to the first time he'd held her and she'd wrapped him around her little finger. He loved all of his children equally, but he'd always felt more protective of his little girl. He wished he could spare her the heartache the truth about her mother might bring.

"Before I start, I want you to know how much I love you."

"I love you, too, Dad." She squeezed his hands. "Now quit stalling." Brows lowering, she fixed him with a stare he recognized. His stare. The one he used to signal he meant business.

"Your biological grandfather was a man named Sam. Eighteen years ago, he showed up on my doorstep out of the blue one night. Sam's daughter was barely twenty and she'd just given birth to a sickly—" his voice hitched "—but so very beautiful baby girl."

"And my father?"

Here was where things started getting tougher.

"He abandoned your mother." He paused for a moment to let that part soak in before continuing. "Your mother was in no position to be a mother. Sam talked her into letting him find a good home for the baby. He said his daughter vowed she loved her baby but knew she couldn't care for a child. He provided documents from both your biological mother and father that signed away their rights to you."

She deflated, tears streaming down her face, her body shaking from the impact of the news. This was a story he wished he never had to burden her with, but he knew she had the right to know. It didn't make the telling any easier, though. He'd give anything to take away the pain snaking its way onto Maya's face. To stop the quiver in her lips.

And his gut knotted since there was still a second shoe to drop once his daughter found out her mother was someone she knew.

"Maya, honey, I'm sorry." He wanted to gather her into a hug and promise everything would be all right, the way he'd done when she was growing up. When she'd trusted him to fight those battles for her. "Sam was drunk three-quarters of the time and had gambled away anything left of the family money."

"But why did he choose you?" The sentence came out in a rasp. A voice of a much younger Maya cracking through as a sob racked her.

It broke him.

"Harrington York—Sterling Perry's father-in-law—willed me a small parcel of land. Land that Sam swore York had promised to him one day. But the land went to me and that was the start of my oil business."

Ryder hated to paint her biological grandfather in a bad light, but Maya wanted to know the truth and he wouldn't lie to her any longer. "Sam harbored a grudge against the Perrys and me because of that. He told me that I owed him for what happened and this was my chance to repay him by making sure the baby was raised by a wealthy family in a closed private adoption."

As much as Ryder had hated the way the man had gone about things, he couldn't let Havery walk out the door with that infant. The man couldn't be trusted. Ryder hadn't cared about anything else but making sure the baby had a good home.

That she felt loved. Damn it, that still was the only thing that mattered to him in all of this.

He took a deep breath and finished the story. "Sam swore that his daughter—Tatiana Havery—didn't want to know where you went."

"Tatiana Havery?" Maya's face crumpled as the name sank in, as she realized that her birth mother was someone who moved in their world and their lives.

Her shoulders shook harder, sobs racking her. Ryder opened his arms and—thank God—she flew into his hug without hesitation to cry it out. A lump lodged in his throat, too, and neither of them said a word until her tears slowed.

Then she eased back, swiping her wrists under her eyes. "Thank you for telling me, Dad. I'm going to need some time to digest all of this."

Feeling helpless to right this for his child, Ryder watched her rush away, her red hair rippling behind her, hair she'd inherited from her mother. Sighing hard, Ryder sagged back in the chair. He hoped he hadn't lost Maya forever for not telling her the truth sooner.

This whole situation had spun out of control so damn quickly. He rubbed a hand over his suit jacket lapel, still damp from his daughter's tears.

He didn't like or trust Tatiana one bit. But she was also Angela's best friend. And he'd been keeping Maya's parentage a secret from her, too, even when they were engaged, since Tatiana herself was unaware that Maya was hers. If Ryder wanted to have a real chance at a future with Angela, he couldn't hold back about that any longer. He just prayed it wouldn't be the end of them.

Time was definitely running out for him to tell Angela that eighteen years ago he'd adopted Tatiana's child. And he had to pray Angela and his daughter would understand.

Because he loved them both too much to lose either of them.

Nine

Drawing Esme toward his bedroom after their dinner at the club, Jesse didn't want anything to ruin their last night together in Royal. She was excited about returning to Houston, though he wasn't sure he shared that excitement.

Hell, who was he kidding? He wasn't happy about her departure at all, even though he would make the trip with her to review the new clubhouse. Having her here on the ranch had felt too damn right, increasingly so every day they spent together. In spite of what she seemed to think, she fit here. From the way she helped with the ranch to how she blended in with the community, she belonged.

And when she'd looked at the children in the club's childcare center with such tenderness and even a hint of longing, his last reservation had slid away. He wanted her to make that audition for the role of wife to be a permanent one. Which meant he would have to persuade her to come back to Royal. If not permanently, at least for a while.

One step at a time.

Closing the door to his suite behind them, he flipped on the sconces near the headboard, dimming them low as he turned to soak in the sight of Esme shouldering off the sleeve of her green velvet dress. She looked so beautiful tonight and for a moment, he let himself be mesmerized by the sight of her undressing, until she stood barefoot in a black lace bra-and-panties set. It had been all he could do to keep his hands off her during dinner.

With careful precision, she laid the green velvet dress over the back of the chaise longue as he shrugged off his jacket. Before he laid it aside, however, he pulled an envelope from the pocket and stepped closer to her. "I have something for you."

"A gift? Thank you." She looked up in surprise as she took off her chandelier earrings, the jewels throwing multicolored prisms onto her creamy skin. "But it isn't Christmas yet. I don't open my presents until the actual day."

Doing nothing more than standing with her jewelry cupped in her delicate, manicured hands, she made his heart beat faster. A blonde goddess set against the warm brown tones of his bed. Where he longed to be with her.

"It's a 'just because' gift, something you'll need before the twenty-fifth." He pulled out two tickets and fanned them between his fingers.

She set aside her earrings on the mahogany chest of drawers. "Tickets?"

Her voice was neutral. Not a good sign, but he pressed ahead all the same.

"To *A Christmas Carol*. Royal may not be Houston, but we have a good community theater. I thought we could go this weekend after we return from Houston."

And he waited.

"I'm surprised." She smiled, stepping into his arms and wrapping her own around his neck. "This is very thoughtful. Thank you."

She kissed him, long and deep, with a familiarity woven from their past two weeks as lovers. The caress of her fingers along the back of his neck was cool, the press of her breasts a sweet temptation against his chest.

Much longer and he would have her against the wall before he'd locked in her return to Royal.

He angled back, stroking her blond hair over her shoulders with a caress down her spine. "Would you rather do something in Houston? I have no problem going back to the drawing board. We could make the plans together."

"You're asking me to come back here for Christmas?" Blue eyes searched his.

He couldn't quite make out the hesitation or confusion he saw brimming in her face. He prided himself on being an adept observer of body language. Except he couldn't hold on to a thought long enough to press his agenda, not with his mind scrambled by Esme's touch, the press of her breasts against his chest.

"Yes, I'm asking you to come back."

"Let's worry about the future later. You're welcome to pamper me right now any other ways that come to mind. I'll be much nicer about accepting your present," she said with an unmistakable invitation in her siren's voice as she tugged him toward the bed, walking backward.

And he didn't need any encouragement to follow, his gaze drawn like a magnet to the sway of her hips. The narrow indent of her waist. The long, smooth line of her thighs. By the time he tumbled with her onto the mattress, he couldn't think about anything but pleasuring her. Making her remember how this connection they shared could burn away everything else.

Tunneling his fingers into her hair, he angled her head to kiss her long and slow, deeply and thoroughly. He took his time lowering the strap of her bra, cupping each breast in turn, savoring the shivers that went through her. He liked the feel of her hands on him as she peeled off his shirt, stripped off his belt.

By the time he moved lower to kiss his way down her shoulder, they were both breathing hard, the whisper of exhales mingling with the slide of fabric across the duvet as they swept away the rest of their clothes. Fevered touches gave way to more demanding kisses. His. Hers.

He felt the taut need in her movements as her hips nudged his thighs. Obliging her unspoken demand, he curved a palm over her hip and traced his way to the juncture of her thighs, and he teased her there.

Fingernails bit into his shoulders, a welcome counterpoint to his own need firing through him. He sensed how close she was to finding her release, so he stayed right with her, whispering into her ear how much he wanted her.

When the soft shudders racked her body, the sense of triumph was almost as fierce as his own desire. He didn't let go for long moments, helping her find every last sweet sensation from her orgasm.

As she stilled, he angled back to glimpse her, to memorize this moment. Her flushed cheeks. Her lips swollen from his kisses. A protective surge fired through him.

He never tired of seeing her in his bed.

Her bed, too, now.

For how long?

He brushed aside the thought that threatened to steal this perfect moment from them both. He refused to accept it could be the last time he had her in his home. Having her stay in Houston was unacceptable.

All the same, there was a frenzy between them tonight. She reached into the bedside table and passed him a condom, urging him to hurry, her voice breathless and encouraging as she sheathed him. Her touch was slow and deliberate. Knowing and tempting.

"Jesse…"

She didn't need to ask him twice.

He rolled her under him in a smooth sweep, sliding inside with a sense of home. Her legs glided up and around his hips, holding him, syncing them both into a perfect rhythm. Flesh against flesh. Heartbeats racing against each other.

They'd made love in every room of his house in every position and still each time with her was as exciting as the first. And while he wasn't a romantic, there was something special between them. Something unique. He would be a fool to let it go. To let her go.

Purring her pleasure, she urged him to his back and straddled him. She rode him, fanning the blaze inside him that begged for release.

His hands dug into her hips, guiding her faster as he thrust upward. Even as his eyes grew heavy with the need to seal in this moment, he couldn't tear his gaze away from the sight of her over him. Her blond hair over her shoulders and along her breasts. Her chest rising and falling faster. Her pale flesh flushing. Her release was close. He knew her body that well now. And seeing her orgasm was the sexiest thing he'd ever experienced.

So much so, it sent him crashing into his own climax, sensation surging through him as he plunged into her. It was more than sex. It was— He stopped the thought short, too dazed to let his mind travel that path. She'd already rocked his world beyond measure in a few short weeks.

His life had been forever changed by the rainstorm that had landed her on his doorstep. And now everything was riding on their trip to Houston and being able to persuade her to leave it all behind.

Because he couldn't imagine his life without her.

Tatiana was seething over the board meeting about to take place, bigwigs from Royal in Houston to represent the charter chapter of the Texas Cattleman's Club.

And she wasn't welcome.

She tried her damnedest to scrub out any trace of the woman she was before she rose to power in Perry Holdings. She'd shed family mementos.

Opted for all new things. Posh designer fixtures. Symbolic, partly, of creating the life she wanted. It still counted for nothing. Got her nowhere. As if not being born into the world of the Perrys meant she could never fully enter the rarefied realm of Houston's wealthiest society.

Angela called herself a friend, but hadn't gotten Tatiana a ticket to the inner circle. No matter how much money she made, how high she rose in the Perry firm, she was still an outsider. She'd never felt that more than today. Her fist clenched around a crystal paperweight. Waterford. For once, though, her designer-decorated town house brought her no comfort. She struggled against the urge to hurl the paperweight through the window.

Instead, she strode over to her white Christmas tree decorated with monochrome lights, with silver tinsel and pale blue ornaments. Normally, the twinkling delighted her. An anchor in an ocean of chaos. Today, even as she straightened the ornaments, Christmas magic held nothing for her.

Her doorbell rang, the high-pitched bell chimes cutting her thoughts short and launching a wave of panic through her. Could it be the police? She had spent the past nine months looking over her shoulder. She wasn't sure how much more of this she could take.

With a deep breath, she steadied her nerves and

scraped her red hair back into a sleek ponytail. Not a strand of hair out of place.

She looked through the peephole.

It wasn't the police. Far from it. A stranger, a teenager, stood in the corridor. Her long red hair and mustard-yellow coat were definitely not cop material, even if she'd been older.

Curious, Tatiana opened the door. "Yes, what can I do for you…"

She let her question drift off, a hint for the teen to introduce herself.

"Maya," she said, jamming her fists into her yellow coat. "My name is Maya Currin."

Currin? Maya Currin, as in Ryder's daughter? Tatiana had heard Angela talk about her future stepdaughter. But other than that, Tatiana had had no contact with the Currin family all these years.

But something brought the girl here today and Maya could use a distraction. "Come in, dear. What can I do for you?"

Maya stepped over the threshold warily, her hyperfocus on Tatiana unnerving. Just as she considered asking the girl to leave, Maya turned her attention to the condo, walking to the massive wall of glass, flattening her palm against it.

"I'm Ryder Currin's youngest. I've been away at college for my freshman year, but I'm home for Christmas."

The girl looked around the apartment, staring unabashedly, her gaze lingering on the white plush sofa.

What the hell was going on? Was the girl unhinged? "Are you looking for someone?"

A shaky sigh rocked through her before she continued. "I've always known I was adopted. My father always swore he would tell me about my biological family once I turned eighteen, but he's been putting it off. Until yesterday, when I insisted." She turned back to Tatiana. "I stayed awake all night working up the nerve to confront you."

Tatiana's scalp tingled with premonition. This conversation couldn't be headed where she thought... Still, she started shaking, staring at this beautiful girl with red hair and brown eyes.

Practically a mini version of her.

Tears misted her eyes as the undeniable truth hit home. "Are you my daughter?"

She didn't even need Maya to respond. She knew. Could sense it between them. Her heart fractured all over again at the time they'd spent apart. And how close her child had been all this time.

Kept from her by Ryder Currin.

Maya nodded slowly. "Yes. My father can confirm it."

Fat tears rolled down Maya's face and she flew into Tatiana's arms with zero hesitation. The one thing that was hers, that no one could take from her. Tatiana held her tight with a possessive urgency. Her child. Grown, safe and beautiful. She'd led the pampered childhood Tatiana hadn't had. If only Maya's childhood hadn't been with that horrid Ryder Currin.

Regret threatened to level her. The choices she'd made had been impossible. Unfair. The reality of how much she'd lost stood in front of her now, a haunting reminder of how truly she'd been robbed.

"I wanted to keep you. I loved you so much." Tatiana held her hands tightly, hardly able to believe she was truly touching her baby girl. "But I had no money. I was alone. My father was on his last legs healthwise." A nice way to gloss over her father's alcoholism. "I begged him to let me give you to a good family to raise."

And her father had promised her he would. Then he'd turned around and given her baby to Ryder Currin. The betrayal cut deeper than any other.

Fury rose in her, only tempered by the joy of meeting Maya.

"Thank you for letting me in and telling me," Maya said. "There are so many questions I want to ask, but I have to get back to my dad. I—I—" The teen stuttered with nerves. "I hope we can get to know each other."

Tatiana's broken heart warmed, and she was filled with pride over this beautiful child she had created. "I would love that."

She hugged her daughter again, transported back

to the day she'd held the infant bundle in her arms, her heart broken, her life wrecked. The memories lingered long after she'd escorted Maya to the door, leaning against the frame to watch her child walk to the elevator, step inside and disappear from view.

Overwhelmed by emotion, Tatiana backed into her condo and leaned against the closed door, unable to think straight. The man she despised was raising the daughter she'd always loved. It wasn't fair. Her whole damn life wasn't fair right now.

For the first time since she'd decorated her apartment, she felt weighed down in this space, in spite of the pristine white decor she'd chosen for a sense of freedom, of a fresh start unsullied by the past. Normally, it soothed her, giving her a sense of control.

Instead, right now the piercing all-white motif made her feel as though she'd been trapped in a hospital, about to undergo surgery. Except the surgery was a painful montage of every moment in her life that went so damn wrong.

She couldn't escape the cornered feeling that her brother might give her up to avoid jail time. The more she thought about it, the more freaked out she became until she surrendered to the fear. Racing around the condo, she threw a haphazard collection into her suitcase, then frantically searched for her passport. She had to leave the country. Now.

But…

How could she? Her daughter, her baby girl, was

here in Houston. And after all this time, she had the chance to get to know her. Her mind whirled all over the place with questions. Had Angela known about this? All this time? That her boyfriend had been raising Tatiana's daughter?

The fury raged. Angela had to have known. The bitch.

Someone had to pay for all Tatiana had been through. Angela had a golden life, full of advantages from being Sterling Perry's child, and now from being with Ryder Currin. Both men disgusted Tatiana. They'd stolen that parcel of land from her father. If he hadn't been cheated, then her family wouldn't have fallen apart. She wanted Sterling and Ryder to hurt as much as she did right now, as much as she'd always hurt when she'd thought of her daughter.

Her fury focused on the perfect way to make both men suffer. By taking from them someone precious. Angela. If Angela were to die…

Tatiana's hand tightened around the paperweight again, the crystal cool in her grip, like a rock in her hand with enough heft to bash in a head. She forced her hold to relax. Whatever happened next was totally in her control.

She'd killed once. She could do so again.

Esme could hardly believe she was back in Houston. Home. And that Jesse was with her.

It seemed like a lifetime ago that she'd left for Royal. So much had changed since then, hell-bent on making a difference for her dad. She still wanted that for him. In fact, she looked forward to seeing the two most special men in her life—Jesse and her dad—making a difference in the club.

Her family, Jesse, even her brother and sisters.

The gathering would be like a family reunion.

Her suede pumps click-clacked musically against the tile floor in the Houston club building. A tour of the facility had gone well, and now they were meeting in a conference room. Every reverberation made her feel more at home, more comfortable with her newfound happiness. As she turned the corner, she saw a familiar silhouette.

Angela dressed with her pitch-perfect fashion sense in a black-and-white A-line dress with a small clutch. Her sister noticed her nearly at the same moment. A wide grin pulled the corners of her mouth skyward.

With determined steps, Esme closed the distance between her and Angela, wrapping her older sister in a tight hug. She'd missed her and wanted to share the latest news about the burgeoning relationship with Jesse. She just knew Jesse and Ryder would enjoy each other's company, too, both such down-to-earth men with a love of the land. So much joy and hope for the future coursed through her heart. But as she eased back and looked more fully at her sister, she could sense something was off with Angela.

"What's going on?" Esme prodded gently. Possibilities cartwheeled through her mind.

At the simple question, Angela's face paled. Deeper concern rose in Esme's chest, and she maneuvered them to one of the decorative palms out of earshot of the people milling in the halls as guests from Royal began arriving at the Houston chapter clubhouse for the tour of the new facility.

A somewhat nervous laugh trembled from Angela's lips. That's when Esme knew something serious had happened. Top of the list of her guesses? "Are you and Ryder okay?"

If that man had hurt her sister again, Esme would never forgive him.

"Well…that's a million-dollar question. I'm still reeling. Prepare yourself. Turns out Maya, Ryder's adopted daughter, is actually Tatiana's daughter. Tatiana. My best friend. And Tatiana never told me." Angela's voice shook. "She never even hinted she gave up a baby. And Ryder… I just… I just can't believe he didn't tell me before now. I'm trying not to feel betrayed. But it's just…a lot of information to digest."

Esme blinked. Then she immediately scanned the room for Ryder Currin, who was deep in conversation with a group of people down the hall. That bastard had actually once been engaged to Angela and hadn't opened up about his life—about something that would have a deep impact on his fiancée. Sure, his children were all adults now, but they would have been Angela's stepchildren, an important connection. He'd expected Angela to give her all to a relationship, yet he'd held back about this tie to her best friend.

And where did that leave them now?

Her sister's breakup with Ryder had been rough. That was no secret. They'd fought for their relationship, though, made it back to a promising forever. But she imagined information like this didn't do a lot in the way of bolstering trust in a relationship that still needed healing.

Esme schooled her features into PR neutrality. The last thing Angela needed was Esme's anger piled on top of all the turmoil she must be feeling. Esme just wanted to be here for her sister. "Are you having second thoughts about being with Ryder?"

Angela wrung her hands until her knuckles turned pale, nerves clearly rising hard and fast. "I know that I love him."

Esme pulled her gaze from her distraught sister to Ryder Currin again. Did the man love Angela as much? Was he the man Angela deserved? He inclined his head to the rancher he chatted with, his black Stetson obscuring his face.

Esme wished she had the answers and assurance. Love was a risky prospect. Even thinking about a future with Jesse was scary—and exciting. There was so much potential for heartbreak and failure. And opportunity for happiness.

She turned back to her sister. "What can I do for you?"

Her sister let out a breath. "Just be here for me. Be my sister." She pressed a trembling hand to her chest, the absence of her engagement ring so very sad. The tan line even remained. Faint, but there, if one looked close enough. "I can't say this hasn't thrown me. I feel like I barely know him."

Throat bobbing, Angela's voice trailed off.

Esme struggled for the right words. Just being there somehow didn't seem like enough. "I realize this is unbelievably hard. I'm here whenever you need to talk."

Never had she been more grateful for her siblings to support one another, to continue the family bond. They needed one another.

Jesse was right that family was everything. And if he moved here, he could share in all of hers.

Esme squeezed Angela's hand in more unspoken support.

"I'll be okay. I'm glad you're home." Angela squeezed back in understanding, the sibling connection never more tangible. Esme felt like finally she and her sister had related without any barrier, no more being an outsider to Angela and Melinda's twin bond.

She wasn't going to let that go and hoped the same progress could be made with Melinda.

Esme made a mental note to talk to her sister more about this later, and they made their way into the conference room. Esme was drawn into a conversation about the press releases she needed to send out while someone tapped Angela with a question about the order of events. Giving her sister one last glance before they parted ways, Esme had to admire Angela's strength through so much adversity.

Then, turning her attention from the influx of people on-site for the meeting, Esme took a moment to admire the renovations. There was still some work to complete before the holiday party a couple of days before Christmas, much less in time for the official opening at the huge New Year's Eve blowout gala.

But it was still already an impressive conference room, from the lengthy wooden table to the massive chairs all around. Crystal pitchers of water were placed strategically, but she was too nervous.

She was actually listening to her first Texas Cattleman's Club business meeting, with all the influential players on hand, including the current Royal chapter president and board members. Familiar faces, new friends even, after her time at Jesse's. Cord and Sheriff Battle sat on either side of her father. Ryder Currin scowled from the other side of the table where he sat with Angela. It saddened Esme that her sister seemed a gulf away, but they would mend that with time. Angela had to understand Esme's reasons for rooting for their father.

Then the gavel sounded, startling Esme and pulling her upright just as the meeting was called to order.

Ten

Echoes of Houston traffic pierced the walls of the historic site of the new Texas Cattleman's Club. One of the many reasons Jesse avoided Houston. Too much traffic. Too many people. Too many buildings.

Not enough sounds of crickets and birdsong. Not enough roaming horses and cattle. Not enough intentional living. He wouldn't even know it was Christmastime here, the only nod to the season the massive tree in the lobby.

He couldn't wait to get Esme back to Royal where they could celebrate the holiday together, under the spruce he'd cut down himself. The one they'd decorated together in front of the fireplace, sharing memories from their childhoods as they did so.

The sooner he finished this meeting, the sooner he could hit the road with her. Jesse hung back in the meeting room, the rest of the board from the Royal chapter seated around the conference table listening to pitches for leadership positions. Leaning against the wall, he studied the players. There were more contenders than just Sterling Perry and Ryder Currin to consider for the role. Venture capitalist Camden McNeal. Or Lucas Ford, an investigator and security mogul. Plus there was a wild card in the mix with Cord Galicia moving from Royal to Houston. He could well be a strong candidate to see the club through the start-up, since he had firsthand experience with the inner workings of the Royal chapter.

Jesse couldn't quite comprehend how his neighbor was going to make big-city life work. Even living on the outskirts of Houston. The hum, bustle and lights of the urban area radiated outward in palpable bands.

Jesse was already feeling claustrophobic, ready to get back home. To take Esme to that Christmas play and continue his campaign to persuade her to move.

Settling his weight onto the heels of his best pair of boots—a thoughtful gift from his sister three

Christmases ago—Jesse scanned the crowd. He attempted to read the reactions of his fellow members. It seemed he was not the only one keeping a tight rein on his emotions during the candidates' speeches. Members listened attentively, doing their part to hear the unique plans each potential president would do his best to execute.

As Ryder Currin finished his pitch to run the new club and returned to his seat beside Angela, Esme took the floor. Apparently, Sterling intended to let his daughter put her PR skills to work and do the talking for him. Jesse worked to keep his face neutral, which was tough to do with Esme using all of her job savvy to lobby for her father. She was poised. Articulate. Convincing.

Damn. This woman enchanted him. Seeing her here today was more proof of her sexy-smart charm. He couldn't even detect a trace of nerves as she adjusted the microphone at the lectern to make herself better heard. Of all the places he'd seen her, she looked like she was born to be in the spotlight.

Crossing his arms over his chest as he leaned against the back wall, he focused on Esme in action. She looked stunning in her sleek black power suit. Her sky-high heels reminded him of meeting her for the first time, her broken shoes sinking into the mud, her beautiful blond hair soaked. She'd been a drowned rat, but somehow managed to keep her composure.

That charisma was in full wattage today, and not just her poise, but her keen mind. Her father watched her with unmistakable pride. Jesse took the measure of the man from a different perspective now, as Esme's dad, rather than just an infamous figure in the news.

Sterling had aged well, his brown hair graying at the temples. His blue eyes were the same shade as Esme's, and he also seemed to share her appreciation of style. His suit had a custom cut, his cowboy boots expensive without even a scuff. He may have worked as foreman of the ranch to prove himself to his father-in-law decades ago, but Jesse doubted Sterling was much of a hands-on ranch owner these days.

He looked 100 percent a powerhouse Texas businessman. And that's how Esme was pitching her dad to the Royal chapter board. As a successful, ambitious entrepreneur who'd expanded beyond just the ranch. Always striving for perfection, her father didn't know the meaning of the word "enough." Perry Holdings included real estate as well as banking, property management and construction.

In fact, Perry Holdings was responsible for the stunning renovations of this very building, with the help of Ethan Barringer, CEO of Perry Construction. Originally from Royal, Ethan made for a nice connection between the two worlds in tackling this project.

Esme painted her father as a visionary who knew how to put together a winning team, this historic building a symbol of his plan to grow the Houston branch of the Texas Cattleman's Club into the future.

In total Perry Holdings PR mode, Esme had them eating out of the palm of her hand.

Jesse realized *this* was the essence of who Esme really was. A city woman. A businesswoman. And no matter how sweet it had been to have her in his bed, in his house—in his life—he couldn't escape the deep-seated sense that eventually she would be miserable out on his ranch, far from the work she obviously did so well.

She completed her presentation and returned to sit beside her father. His smile of appreciation and pride brought a light to Esme's eyes. Even her sister nodded approval during the applause from across the room.

Esme blinked fast, a sheen of tears in her eyes. She was clearly choked up. Emotional.

She'd warned him about that, about her romantic side. She had a heart that was easily touched, and he'd grown to appreciate that about her. But how could he justify taking Esme from these people she loved? He recognized how selfish it would be. From a job she was born to perform. His freshly formed dreams of building a life with her at his side faded. He cared for her too much. His heart ached already at the thought of saying goodbye. But he wanted her to have the life that would make her happy.

Unable to take another moment of this meeting, Jesse ducked out into the hall, his focus homed in on the exit, on getting away from there as quickly as possible. Just as he reached the door, he heard the sound of fast-clicking high heels on the floor, growing closer.

"Jesse," Esme called. "Jesse, where are you going?"

He turned in the lobby—empty save for a towering Christmas tree—and the sight of her glowing smile poleaxed him. He swallowed down a lump in his throat, unable to push past the emotion.

She reached him and rested her palm on his chest. "What did you think of my presentation? I really think it went well, but I don't want to be overly optimistic. Still, I think a celebration is in order. Dinner out at my favorite Houston hot spot. My treat."

She looked so happy. So hopeful. The knowledge ate away at him.

"Esme." He clasped her hand and removed it from his chest. "I have something to tell you."

Her smile faded as she glanced down at the way their hands were suspended in air. "You look serious. Is something wrong?"

Everything. He'd made a huge mistake thinking he could change her, that he could transplant her to his world and mold her into the kind of woman he'd always imagined at his side. To do that would be a disservice to the bright, beautiful, smart woman she was.

So even though it hurt like hell, he forced himself to say the words that would send her out of his life for good. The quicker the better. Rip that bandage right off. He did his best to take a page out of her book. Keep his tone neutral. Final. Definitive. Sure. "I've made my decision about a wife candidate. And I'm sorry, but it's not you."

Her gasp of surprise cut through the silence between them. Shock froze her features, followed by a wash of pain in her eyes at his rejection of all they'd shared over the past couple of weeks. That glimpse into her heart damn near broke his, but he told himself she would be happier this way.

Living her own dreams instead of his.

Then her shoulders went back, her chin tipped with pride. A feral smile brushed over her lips though pain shone in her pretty blue eyes. "Congratulations," she said bitterly. "I'm glad you got exactly what you wanted."

She adjusted her jacket, sweeping her blond locks over her shoulders. Without another word, she brushed past him, striding past the towering Christmas tree and out the door.

And out of his life.

* * *

Weary, physically and emotionally, Angela punched in the code to her condominium. Latches releasing, she pushed inside, ready to put the events of the last twenty-four hours behind her. Far, far behind her. She needed space and a moment to breathe and process. Once inside, she dropped her purse on the floor and reached to turn on the lights.

She startled in surprise, the shock followed by a twinge of fear. Someone was huddled on her sofa. Fear slammed into her chest and constricted her breathing. She'd seen enough crime shows to know victims usually had a small, narrow window of escape. She reached for the doorknob behind her, quietly...

Then recognized the female curled up on her couch among the holiday throw pillows and sighed in relief. Her jagged heartbeat returning to normal, she laid a hand on her chest, her linen dress rough against her fingertips. "Esme, you scared me for a moment."

Her youngest sister looked up, her eyes red from crying as she hugged a red velvet throw pillow with a silver embroidered reindeer. "I hope you don't mind that I used your spare key. I couldn't bear to be alone."

Fresh sobs rolled out of Esme. Her normally perfect makeup was smeared across her face. She looked so different from the woman who had just delivered a fiery and impassioned speech on behalf of her father. Something was seriously wrong for Esme to display such unfettered emotion.

Worry filling her, Angela crossed into the living room and nudged aside the ceramic snowman to reach the box of tissues on the coffee table. "What's wrong?"

Esme drew in a ragged breath, gripping the velvet pillow tassels. "It's over between Jesse and me."

Angela's eyebrows raised in surprise. But then she pushed aside her thousand questions to be there for her sister. Reaching a protective arm around her sister, she gripped Esme in a side hug. "Oh, sis, I'm so sorry."

"We haven't even known each other long." Her face was lined with pain. "It shouldn't hurt this much."

"Our hearts aren't tied to time." She understood too well about love and heartbreak because of her rocky relationship with Ryder. Angela stroked her sister's shoulder, attempting to soothe her as much as she could.

Wishing she could take her pain away.

Losing their mother early on had forced them to be close. And Angela was grateful for that closeness. But at times like this, her heart ached for their mother. What would Tamara have said to soothe Esme? To soothe Angela, even? She tipped her head closer to Esme's, doing her best to comfort.

Clutching a tissue, Esme blew her nose. Tears

still leaked down her face. In a cracked tone, she continued.

"Thank you for understanding, for not writing me off as histrionic."

"Of course not. I'm glad you reached out to me. You shouldn't be alone." She plucked another tissue from the box and passed it over.

Her cell phone rang from her purse back at the door. She glanced at it, but looked away fast, not wanting her sister to feel like she had anything other than Angela's full attention. It was rare that Esme showed vulnerability to her. She had always seemed a bit jealous of Angela and Melinda's bond.

Esme dabbed at her eyes. "Please take the call. It'll give me a chance to pull myself together."

"If you're sure…" Angela hesitated.

"Absolutely." She nodded, standing and grabbing her purse.

"Okay, then, but I'll make it quick. Don't go anywhere." She retrieved her own purse and fished out her phone. Her eyes scanned the screen. Tatiana? Angela still hadn't quite wrapped her brain around the fact that her friend had given up a baby for adoption and never told her about it. She would have wanted to help, even if just to listen. Maybe that's what this call was about.

She answered. "Hello, Tatiana, what can I do for you?"

"Angela, I need you." Tatiana sobbed hard on the other end of the phone.

She bit the bullet and plunged right in, her gut telling her the timing of Tatiana being this upset couldn't be a coincidence after Ryder's conversation with his youngest child. "Is this about Maya Currin...about your daughter?"

"Yes," Tatiana whispered. "That's exactly what this is about. And I really need to talk to you. Everything is so out of control. My half brother's in prison and he's clearly mentally unstable. He's been threatening to say all sorts of awful things about me."

"I'm so sorry you're going through that. Let's meet for breakfast in the morning."

Tatiana hiccuped on another sob. "I need to talk to you now. In person."

Angela glanced to her still-hurting sister standing at the kitchen counter wiping her tears around her eyeliner. Shaking her head, she answered her friend. "I'm afraid I—"

Esme turned, her brave face on. "It's okay. Go. I know she's your friend and it's okay."

"But you're my sister." She wanted to be with Esme. To find out why things had ended so quickly between her and a man she'd been so excited about.

"Thank you," Esme said with a watery smile. "How about we go over together?"

Angela nodded, relieved not to be torn between

her sister and her friend. Of course she would choose Esme, but with Willem in jail, Tatiana didn't have any family left.

Other than Maya.

Her heart pinched at the thought. "Tatiana, Esme and I can come over right now. Just let us know where you are."

Angela reached for a notepad and jotted down the location and time. The new club. In a half hour. So simple, she wondered why she'd bothered to write it. She was such a jumble of emotions today.

But it helped take her mind off her own relationship to be there for others.

Angela ended the call and turned to her sister. "We can talk in my car on the way over." Then she grabbed her purse and went to the door.

Esme followed close on her heels. "Getting to be with you helps. Even if we don't talk. I just don't want to be alone right now."

Taking Esme at her word, when Angela got to her car, she turned on soft Christmas carols. Esme sat silently beside her, her head resting against the window, her sniffles further and further apart.

Angela's cell phone rang a couple of times with calls from Ryder, but she wasn't ready to talk to him, not yet. The third time he called, she sent him straight to voice mail and turned off her cell. She couldn't handle another emotional conversation sidetracking her tonight. It felt like the whole world was falling apart.

A half hour later, Angela pulled up outside the back entrance of the club, the historic building rather foreboding at night. While Christmas lights lined the street and lit up the other buildings, the club was pitch-black inside, the only illumination a Christmas tree in the lobby. She was glad she'd brought someone along with her. Tatiana's car was parked in back, too, so she had to be inside the building already. Why would she be sitting in the dark?

Arriving at the back door, Angela tapped in the security code, something Tatiana would know, too, since she was with Perry Holdings.

"Tatiana," Angela called as she walked inside, her sister following a step behind.

A faint light shone from the back parlor, the dim glow giving the place a creepy vibe that reminded her that the body of the murdered Perry Holdings assistant had been found in this building. Of course she had to think of that now, when she was already uneasy.

"Tatiana?" she called again, reaching for a switch to flip on the lights.

Tatiana stepped into view, her red hair in wild disarray. A step closer and she was bathed in light.

And her arms were extended, a gun held with steady hands.

Esme gasped behind her. Shocked and confused, Angela couldn't figure out what her friend was doing.

Tatiana waved the gun, gesturing toward the parlor. "Both of you. In there."

What the hell was going on? Was Tatiana unhinged? Angela cast a quick glance at her stunned sister. She wasn't sure how they were going to get out of this, but she had to believe they would figure something out.

Angela kept her voice low even though her heart pounded so very hard with fear. She needed to stay calm. Stay in control of her emotions and de-escalate the situation. Giving herself completely over to fear would only immobilize her. Which might interfere with any way to keep her and Esme safe.

Her hands clenching so hard her nails cut into her palms, Angela struggled for the right words for a situation she never could have imagined happening. "Tatiana, my friend, whatever you're feeling, I understand—"

"Shut up," Tatiana shouted.

Angela snapped her jaw shut. She tried to get a read on the events quickly spiraling out of control. The woman who stood before them might as well have been a stranger. Her expression, her tone, her actions… Angela didn't recognize any of them.

"You're not my friend, Angela, and you can't

have any clue what I'm feeling, or what I've been through. Showing up here with your sister when I said I needed you? You've just proven what I already knew. Perrys always look out for Perrys and to hell with the rest of us."

Fear for her sister constricted her throat.

If only she hadn't brought Esme along, she wouldn't be in danger. "Esme has nothing to do with whatever grudge you have against me. It's not fair to keep her—"

Tatiana closed herself inside the empty parlor with them, the gleam in her eyes vicious. "Nothing in my life has been fair. My father lost everything because the land he was promised by your grandfather went to that idiot Ryder Currin instead. And your sister Melinda gets to have a baby when I had to give up mine."

Tatiana Havery was a madwoman, and Angela had never seen it. Never known. She felt stupid and foolish, all the more so because she couldn't focus on getting out of this situation. Panic clogged her airways, making it hard to breathe.

Esme took a step forward with the signature calm that stood her in good stead at work. "What can we do to make this right for you now?"

She was buying them time. Angela looked around the room, taking in the high windows and lack of furnishings. Tried to formulate a plan that didn't end in death and gunshots. And so far, she came up empty.

She wanted Ryder. Why hadn't she taken his call in the car? If something happened to her and she never got to speak to him again… The hurt of that made her legs wobble beneath her.

Tatiana's gaze swung wildly to her. "It's too late. I thought I was going to get my revenge by bringing down the Perrys and Currins for taking what was rightfully my father's. Yes, I was responsible for spreading all those rumors with the help of my brother. And it was working, too." She pointed the gun back and forth between them. "But then that stupid Vincent Hamm overheard one of our conversations. So I had to kill him."

Angela swallowed down a knot of horror as she looked around and realized that Tatiana had brought them to this building, where Hamm's body had been dumped, with a grisly purpose. And there was nothing in this empty room to defend herself with. She gripped her purse harder, trying to remember what was inside, what might be used as a weapon, all the while trying to keep track of what Tatiana was saying.

"I tried to pin the murder on your father but of course Mr. 'Teflon' Perry got away with it. The Perrys and Currins get everything and my family got nothing. That land would have given my dad a fresh start."

But Tatiana's father had lost everything because of his addiction. He'd gone broke just as Tatiana finished boarding school. She must have had her baby not too long after that.

"Tatiana," Esme said softly, "I remember your dad. We were all so sad when he died in that accident. It had to have been hard for you."

"Accident?" Tatiana shrieked. "It wasn't an accident. He killed himself. Because of your family... and that vile Ryder Currin, who got the land my father should have had. And now Ryder has my daughter, too?"

Esme backed up a step, no longer the conciliatory, smooth businesswoman.

Angela agreed. Talking wasn't going to work. Tatiana was crazed, her speech dripping with bitterness and hatred. She had already made up her mind to murder them.

Angela's purse slid from her shoulder, hitting the floor with a thud. Her cell phone skittered out, a reminder of all those missed calls from Ryder. She would give anything to hear his voice one more time. But she was never going to see Ryder again, never have the chance to hold him, tell him how much she loved him.

She reached for Esme's hand, needing to feel her sister's presence. Wanting to offer whatever love and comfort she could.

Tatiana's face spread in an evil smile. "It's time

Sterling Perry and Ryder Currin learn what it feels like to have their hearts torn out by losing what's dearest to them."

Eleven

Ryder tossed his uneaten supper in the sink.

The dish clanked, the sound jarring in his too-still, too-quiet home on Currin Ranch.

Damn it, he was tired of being ignored. He'd phoned Angela repeatedly since the meeting ended and she wasn't answering. She hadn't called back, much less sent a text in response to his voice mails.

Angela was going to have to talk to him eventually, so it might as well be now. The longer silence stretched between them, the tougher it would be to bridge that gap.

Sure, she'd sat at his side during the meeting, but other than that, she hadn't spoken to him since he'd told her about Tatiana being Maya's biological mother. Angela hadn't even allowed him to apologize for keeping the secret from her. She'd just walked away, refusing to talk to him.

He could see how it would seem that he didn't trust her not to tell Tatiana—her best friend—where her baby had gone. He couldn't help but wonder if he'd kept the information from her because on some level, he had still been holding back from committing.

Whatever the reason, he owed her an apology. They had been engaged. He should have honored that commitment he'd made to Angela. It hadn't been fair to expect her to build a relationship with Maya without all the facts.

He stalked to the foyer to snag his jacket and pluck his keys out of the carved wood bowl in the entryway. He pulled open the door and stopped short. Maya stood on the other side, her keys in hand.

Given how upset she'd been, he hadn't expected to see her so soon. Except she didn't look at all distressed. In fact, she had a hopeful gleam in her tired eyes. All that emotion in a short time must have been draining.

She pushed past him into the house, turning back to him, tentative but with a growing excitement building. "Guess what?"

Shrugging, he tried to imagine. A boy, maybe?

Final grades were posted and she made the president's list? Anything was possible. "I haven't a clue."

"I went to see my birth mother," she blurted. "I told her I'm her daughter."

He went cold inside. He'd figured she would want to meet Tatiana, but he hadn't thought it would happen this soon, before she really had the chance to think through all the implications of the meeting. To prepare herself for her birth mother's potential reactions. He wanted Maya to be happy, but he also wanted to protect her from hurt. What if Tatiana didn't want Maya in her life?

Although based on the happiness on his daughter's face, it seemed the meeting had gone well. "What did Tatiana say?"

"She was so shocked." Maya's hands moved a million miles a minute as she spoke. "She definitely had no idea that you were raising her biological daughter."

It had been her own family's stipulation. Ryder had kept it a secret for good reason.

"And?" Questions piled up inside him, blanketed with a deep sense of foreboding. He could never place his concern, but something about Tatiana had always sent his senses skidding.

"She was glad to meet me. She said she'd never stopped loving me. She cried." Maya swiped away a fresh stream of tears rolling down her cheeks. "She seemed happy, but something in her face made me really believe she regretted the decision, too, you know? Like maybe she'd begged her dad not to send me away? She seemed so overwhelmed, I decided to give her some space to digest."

Thinking of Tatiana's pain sent his thoughts spiraling. His daughter continued to share information about the meeting, but Ryder lost track of her words as bits and pieces of what had happened over the past several months swirled through his head. Vincent Hamm's death. His employee Willem Inwood going to prison for his role in a Ponzi scheme, a scheme he'd attempted to blame on Sterling Perry.

Decades of controversy over that one damn piece of land Harrington York had willed to Ryder, but both Sterling Perry and Sam Havery thought was rightfully theirs. The land had proved to be rich in oil, stoking the bitterness Perry and Havery harbored.

And the oddest piece in this whole puzzle. Inwood was Tatiana's half brother. Ryder had thought it strange Inwood would do something that could jeopardize Tatiana's position at Perry Holdings. But what if they had been colluding to get back at both Ryder and Sterling because of that land?

He could feel the blood drain from his face as he wrapped his brain around the possibility—probability—that Tatiana could have orchestrated those rumors to avenge what happened to her father. For having to give up her baby since she couldn't offer her a future.

An even more horrifying prospect occurred to him. Could she have even killed Vincent?

No. That was a stretch. This was Angela's best friend he was talking about…

Oh God. Angela.

He focused on his daughter again. "Maya, kiddo, I am so glad you're happy." He didn't even want to think of what it would do to his daughter if it turned out her newly found biological mother was a criminal. "I want to hear all about it. But I need to take care of some quick business. Will you wait for me here?"

"Sure, Dad." She backed away, smiling. "It's okay, really. I have tons of things I want to write in my diary so I don't forget anything about this day."

She faded from sight in a flurry of teenage energy and red hair. A surge of protectiveness shot through him. For her. For Angela.

Heaven help anyone who tried to harm his family.

Gathering his keys and wallet, he tried to call Angela again. It went straight to voice mail. He tried Melinda's number, willing her to pick up.

"Hello?" she said, her voice so like Angela's, a shared twin timbre. "What's going on, Ryder?"

His boots ate up the space to the garage. "Is Angela with you? She's not answering her cell and I need to talk to her."

"No, she's not, but I'm at my condo with Slade packing up a few last things before I sell the place." Melinda's condo was in the same building as Angela's. "Do you want me to go check on her?"

"Yes, please."

"I'll call you back from her place if she's not there."

"Thank you." He didn't want to worry Melinda, given her pregnancy, but he also didn't want to waste a minute more.

Waiting for her to phone back felt like an eternity. He threw open the door of his truck and settled behind the wheel, ready to tear out of there if he needed to start a search.

His cell rang from where he'd placed it on the dash. Melinda. He jabbed the screen before the second tone could chime.

"Did you find her?" he asked without preamble.

"She's not here, Ryder." Melinda's answer ramped up his concern. "But I found a note she left behind about some kind of meeting? It says, 'T at the TCC building at 8 p.m.' Does that make any sense to you?"

His grip tightened on the steering wheel. He didn't want to believe the worst. But he knew in his gut, Angela was in grave danger. "Thank you, Melinda. You've been a big help."

Without a second to waste, he peeled out of the garage. Plowing down the drive, he called for backup to meet him at the club.

Houston police detective Zoe Warren.

Royal sheriff Nathan Battle, who, thank God, was still in town.

Ryder knew they wouldn't question him or write off his suspicions the way someone on the other end of a 911 call might. And sure enough, they agreed without hesitation. Zoe had been with Cord and Jesse, who were coming, as well.

The drive felt like an eternity even though he knew he'd made it in half the usual time. Pulling up behind the TCC building, Ryder didn't know whether to be relieved or horrified to find Angela's car parked beside another vehicle. Tatiana Havery's?

Two more cars swept in, doors opening, as his backup arrived. Sheriff Battle raised a finger to his mouth for silence, then motioned for them to follow him.

Ryder's heart raced as they entered the building, fast and silent, everything inside him telling him he needed to get to Angela. Now.

Muffled voices echoed down the corridor, female voices. Coming from the parlor.

Ryder bit back bile while the group crept closer. He kept his footfalls quiet as he picked his way forward, praying there wouldn't be a squeaky floorboard. The voices grew louder, more distinctive.

Tatiana.

Angela.

And Esme?

Nothing about this scene made sense to him. How had it gotten to this point? How had Angela found herself in the crosshairs?

Another rolling wave of protective urges washed over his body. He needed to make sure Angela—and Esme—made it out alive. And in one piece.

Ryder shot a quick look at Jesse Stevens, the Royal rancher who was Cord's close friend. His face was pale, his jaw flexing.

But he looked every bit as hell-bent on getting to the women as Ryder.

The door had a vintage stained glass inset. Shadows moved on the other side, muffled sounds seeping through...

"The Perrys and Currins have to pay for what they did to my father. To me. To my child."

Tatiana.

Every muscle in Ryder tensed for action. He burned to push through that door now and to hell with caution.

Zoe paused, holding up a hand for them to wait. Nathan Battle nodded. This was Zoe's jurisdiction. Her case. Her bust. But Ryder intended to be right on her heels.

Nathan's lips thinned as he checked his weapon. Tension was so thick that it was tangible in the air.

Withdrawing her weapon, Zoe mouthed silently, "One, two…three."

They moved as one, bursting into the room. Ryder's hungry gaze devoured the sight of Angela. Alive.

And held at gunpoint.

"Tatiana," Ryder called, distracting her for a split second, willing to risk taking a shot without hesitation. Angela's life was at stake.

That second's distraction was all it took for Zoe and Nathan to tackle Tatiana while Jesse pushed the two sisters out of the way of any potential gunfire. A single shot went wild and shattered the stained glass.

Then silence.

Sulfur from the gunfire tinged the air.

Adrenaline burned through Ryder as he braced a hand against the wall to keep from sinking to his knees in relief. Angela was safe. Thank God, she was safe. Only a couple of strides away.

"My daughter," Tatiana whimpered as Zoe handcuffed her, reading Tatiana her rights. Glass crunched under their feet on the way out, Tatiana's sobs growing fainter.

But Ryder didn't have the least bit of sympathy for her and didn't intend to waste so much as a single thought for her. His focus was on Angela, barely registering Nathan and Jesse helping Esme to her feet.

Ryder reached for Angela, hauling her close, his heart slamming against his rib cage. "Thank God you're all right. I was so damn scared when I couldn't reach you."

The memory of that interminable drive to the club sucker punched him all over again. He knew with certainty he loved this woman deeply.

"How did you know where to find me? Find us?" Angela looked over at Esme deep in conversation with Nathan Battle. Her sister's arms moved in sweeping gestures, no doubt recounting the story of how they'd wound up at gunpoint. A story he, too, wanted to hear.

An unexpected distance gaped between Esme and Jesse. Maybe they hadn't been as close as everyone thought and it had only been a fling.

Ryder buried his face against the top of Angela's head and breathed in the scent of her shampoo, like an exotic flower. "You left your note with the address and time at your place."

"I'm so glad you made it in time," she whispered, trembling in his arms. "I really believe she would have killed my sister and me."

And if Melinda hadn't discovered that little scrap of paper, he could have lost Angela forever, a blow his heart couldn't have withstood. How could he have let her get away before? Their broken engagement was the biggest mistake of his life.

One he didn't intend to repeat. He would do

whatever it took to win her back. To build a life with her. A strong partner, his lover, his love.

With Angela's help, he would need to tread gently with Maya about her birth mother and what had happened over the past months, culminating in the most horrifying night of his life.

Unwinding the events of the last few hours would take patience and finesse. Traits he deeply admired in the woman he loved. The one who made his life so much better.

His eyes held hers. Throat bobbing, he strung together words. Knowing it would never be enough to explain how he felt about her.

"Angela, you have to know I love you. I've known love before and this is the real thing. Something worth cherishing. And I'll be damned if I'll throw that away again. We're the forever deal. And whatever I need to do to convince you to marry me—"

She pressed her fingers to his mouth, her eyes on him. "Ryder, stop." She eased her hand away. "You don't have to convince me. I love you, too. I want nothing more than to be your wife."

A swell of relief filled him. Along with gratitude for this second chance with Angela.

He pulled out the engagement ring he'd given Angela, a ring he'd kept with him since the day she'd taken it off. "I've kept this with me even

though I was the one who called off our engagement. I couldn't seem to let it go, to let *you* go."

"And now you never have to." She smiled up at
him, her hand outstretched for him to slide the ring
back in place.

Where it would stay for a lifetime.

A week later, Esme stood in the middle of what
she'd once thought would be her dream come true—
a holiday party held at the beautifully renovated
building for the Houston branch of the Texas Cattleman's Club. Tomorrow was Christmas Eve. At
the very least, she should be celebrating having survived Tatiana's attack.

She truly was grateful for her family's safety,
her father's cleared name. Still, the revelry echoed
hollowly around her without Jesse by her side. But
she hadn't heard even a word from him since Tatiana held her and Angela hostage.

A harp played Christmas songs as Texas Cattleman's Club guests from both Houston and Royal
filled the room to celebrate the completed renovations. The formal grand opening was scheduled to
ring in the New Year, the entire memberships of
both chapters invited. Would Jesse attend? Would
she have to see him with whatever "perfect" woman
he'd chosen? The thought sent her stomach plum-
meting. Thankfully, so far, he was a no-show tonight.

The attack had drawn Ryder and Angela closer, though. Angela had gone through so much heartache over the last year that this warmed Esme's soul for her. They were so rock solid these days. Things had been difficult for Maya, but Ryder's older two children had been a wall of support, perhaps having gained strength from their own happiness. His son, Xander, who'd mourned the loss of a fiancée two years ago, had even found love again with cowgirl tomboy Frankie Walsh.

She stepped aside for waitstaff walking by with a silver tray of bacon-wrapped prawns, another carrying flutes. Even the champagne didn't tempt her. While she was happy for her sister, watching the in-love couple reminded her of a very real absence in her own life. The pain was made more palpable when Cord and Zoe romantically sipped from each other's champagne flutes.

The jabs to her heart just kept coming.

Cupping her crystal glass of sparkling water, she tucked herself farther away from the partiers. She needed to put in an appearance for her family's sake, but she wanted to remain as inconspicuous as possible. She'd even chosen her clothes with just that in mind, settling on a basic black cocktail dress. Her only nod to the party and the season was her red Gucci heels.

She was still raw inside from Jesse's rejection, heartbroken in a way that grew more painful every day. She felt adrift. After the vibrant days on Jesse's ranch, she found city life noisy and crowded. Even her job felt soulless now that she'd moved beyond seeking her daddy's approval.

Maybe she should buy a ranch of her own, work in philanthropy like her sister Melinda. Her sister might even welcome her help as Melinda's pregnancy progressed. She could spend more time with her husband, Slade.

Esme pressed her palm to her forehead, her thoughts all over the place. She had no idea what to do with her future, couldn't even think straight. She'd been so hopeful she and Jesse could build a life together. Seeing him walk away after the police hauled off Tatiana had been the worst pain she'd ever endured. He'd meant what he'd said about not wanting her.

How could things be so awful and perfect at the same time? Her father and Ryder were continuing to strengthen their reconciliation, much to Angela's joy. Their dad had even managed to repay the investors who'd panicked and lost so much money, an empathetic move that had people wondering if Sterling had become more than an empty suit after all.

After all the bad blood between the two families, it still felt surreal to Esme that her brother, Roarke, was engaged to Ryder's older daughter, Annabel.

Perry Construction CEO Ethan Barringer and his fiancée, Aria, were deep in conversation with

Liam Morrow and socialite Chloe Hemsworth, both engaged couples radiating such happiness it made Esme ache all over again. An animated Paisley Ford held court with both of them, no doubt sharing news of the latest wedding fashion from her boutique. Her husband, Lucas, smiled proudly, as supportive of his wife as she was of him.

It seemed the whole room was full of couples, making her recent breakup all the more difficult to bear.

Venture capitalist Camden McNeal, his new bride, Vivianne, at his side, had his phone out showing everyone who would look the family photos of the two of them with their toddler daughter. Esme thought of the childcare center in the Royal TCC building, a benefit the Houston chapter didn't offer. She would have never thought to miss it before knowing Jesse and hearing his plans and yearning for a family.

"Can I get you a refill?"

Her father's voice startled her from her pity party. She hated feeling so morose but couldn't seem to shake herself out of it. "Thanks, Dad. I'm good."

He adjusted his tie, ever the clotheshorse. "You really did a top-notch job over in Royal on behalf of our chapter."

"But I didn't do anything that secures the presidency for you. It's still up in the air who'll lead this chapter."

"I can't deny that I would like the position, but I'm okay with however things shake out." He reached for his whiskey glass and finished off the last swallow without even a wince. "You made all of us look good in Royal and laid the groundwork for a great relationship between us."

The two clubs had worked together to draw up nomination papers for board positions and officers, creating the new club's rules and regulations.

His praise meant a lot to her. "Thanks, Dad. I'm glad you're pleased. But I'm not sure what I did."

"Houston and Royal are two very different towns. Forging a strong tie could have been rocky. But you've helped all of us—in both cities—form new business connections and new friendships."

Uncomfortable with praise she wasn't sure she'd earned, she shook her head emphatically. Pieces of her upswept hair loosened, tumbling in front of her eyes. Coming undone, for a change, gave her strange comfort. "It wasn't as difficult as you make it sound. We aren't really that different, Dad."

"If you believe that, then what's kept you from going back to Royal and that man you're obviously so taken with?"

She stared at him incredulously, surprised he'd noticed. She found herself aching to confide in her father, even knowing he couldn't fix this for her. "Dad, he doesn't want me."

"Huh, could have fooled me. Whenever he

looked your way, he seemed besotted." He placed his hands on her shoulders. "And even if he's on the fence about committing, when did a child of mine ever back down without a fight?"

She stared back into her father's eyes, the same color as hers, and let his words sink in, really sink in. About Royal and Houston being similar. About fighting for what she wanted.

He continued, "I made the mistake of paying more attention to business than to my marriage and I paid the price for that. So have you kids. Learn from my mistakes."

The rare glimpse of vulnerability in her father touched her heart and pushed aside barriers of her own making. She'd enjoyed her time at Jesse's ranch, working alongside him, riding to check the cattle, watching sunsets together on his porch.

Dreams spun into possibility. Esme Perry—a wife, a mother, an entrepreneur. Maybe she could have the best of both worlds by working remotely. Why had she gotten it into her head that she had to wait to establish her career before even considering motherhood? They could also share in the Texas Cattleman's Club world and she would still be connected to her family.

She arched up on her toes to kiss her dad on the cheek, a plan to woo Jesse already forming in her mind. "Thanks, Dad. Do you mind if I borrow that old truck of yours I used to learn to drive? I think my Christmas plans just changed."

"Sure," he answered without hesitation. "Just remember, even restored, that sucker's got a tricky clutch."

With a final look at the room full of her family and friends, at the stunning renovations now complete and the club ready to launch, Esme felt her world settle into place. She would always enjoy Houston, but her heart was in Royal now.

She had fallen head over heels in love with Jesse Stevens. And damn straight, Perrys fought for what they wanted.

The night was still young. If she made good time, she could be in Royal to celebrate Christmas Eve with Jesse.

Jesse was decidedly lacking in the holiday spirit, in spite of his decked-out house. The decorations only served as a reminder of all he'd left behind in Houston and how he would be spending Christmas Eve alone. He'd called his sister, exchanged holiday greetings, but then she was off to enjoy her vacation.

Why in the hell he'd thought coming to the stables would be better was beyond him. Esme had permeated every part of his world until there was nowhere to step without thinking of her, wanting her. Ghosts of their time together whispered from every corner of his ranch. And he had no idea how to find peace with her absence.

The familiar scents and sounds of his stable at

night did little to soothe his restless spirit. He just kept thinking of how he would want to share the moment with Esme.

He stroked Duke's nose, wishing those wise brown eyes could offer him some wisdom. "Well, boy, I've made a mess of things, haven't I?"

The horse whinnied in response, shaking his mane. When he was a kid, he used to do this with Apollo. Tell his horse his secrets, dreams, regrets. The act steadied him. At least, a bit.

"I'm already regretting my decision to let her go." He couldn't sleep. He couldn't eat. His life was empty without her. "This ranch means nothing to me without her."

Never had he imagined a moment where the ranch felt like it wasn't enough for him. Sure, he appreciated his horses, his house, the rolling grounds. But he couldn't help but notice its expanse. How big it was. How empty it was.

Pawing the ground, Duke swung his head toward a mare in the next stall. The Appaloosa mare nickered softly.

Everyone was partnering up. Horses included, it seemed. "I want what my married friends at the Texas Cattleman's Club have. A sense of belonging to a family."

That hadn't changed. He just wanted it all with Esme.

Duke nuzzled Jesse on the shoulder. Those

brown eyes stared back at him, catching him up short.

He knew the horse couldn't answer. Not really. Still, the flick of Duke's ear let him know he was listening. Stroking the horse's neck, he kept replaying the memory in his mind of meeting Esme. Of all that life with her seemed to promise. Of all that he'd thrown away.

Jesse's mind circled back around to how this ranch meant nothing without her. How he'd wanted that family with Esme. And everything clicked into place with startling clarity.

For some lame-ass reason, he'd thought that he could only have his dream family here in Royal.

As he rocked back on his boot heels, taking in his stable, thinking about his ranch, he also thought about the club here and the branch starting in Houston. And he realized the heart of that organization beat in either location.

Friends. Family. Community. Home wasn't about a building, or even a plot of land. It was about loving people and having them return that love.

It was still a few minutes shy of Christmas Eve, but there was nothing to say he couldn't make his holiday miracle happen now.

After shooting off a text with instructions for his foreman, Jesse made fast tracks outside, toward the house. He could be packed and on the road in less than ten minutes, but even that felt like an eternity.

Ten minutes later, he settled behind the wheel, a thermos of coffee beside him for the nighttime trip to Houston. Only a few hours separated him and Esme.

Mind made up, he turned the ignition key. He was ready for the journey. He needed to see her. To fight for her. The woman who made every room and space light up with energy and love. He'd been a fool to cast that aside, but he wouldn't let that get in the way of winning her back and healing her heart.

Just as he hit the gas, headlights shone in the distance, barreling down the long drive toward him. He scratched his head, frustrated at what might be a delay. He wasn't expecting anyone.

The vehicle stopped in front of him, his eyes taking a moment to adjust to the bright lights from what appeared to be a restored classic truck with a big red bow on the grille. He held up a hand, blotting out the glare as the door was flung open and a pair of shapely long legs stepped out.

A woman wearing sky-high red leather heels.

Jesse put his truck in Park, a smile building inside and spreading to his face. His heart slugged in his ears, each beat an echo of her name.

Esme.

He didn't know what she was doing in a vintage truck, a magnificent ride that at another time he would have been jonesing to drive. It was on the complete opposite end of the spectrum from her Porsche.

But then, everything about this woman was unpredictable. Perfectly so. He wouldn't have her any other way.

He hit the ground running, his strides eating up the space between them as she ran into his arms, leaping into his embrace. He spun her around, his face buried in her hair, the scent and feel of her filling his senses just as she filled his life.

Easing her to the ground, he sealed his mouth to hers and she met his kiss fully, her hands on either side of his face. No hesitation. He didn't know why she'd forgiven him. He was just glad to his soul that she had.

Jesse skimmed a final kiss over her lips before angling back, enjoying the way the stars were reflected in her eyes. "Nice ride."

"Turns out I'm a fan of trucks and a certain cowboy." She tapped his Stetson.

"And I'm a fan of you." He ran his hand down her sleek blond hair, burying his fingers in the silken strands. "I was just coming to you, but I'm glad we don't have to wait any longer. Every day without you has been miserable. I've been a brooding mess since you left."

"Oh, Jesse," she sighed, looping her arms around his neck. "I've—"

"Shhh." He kissed her quiet. "I need to speak

first, especially after you took such a leap to drive all the way here. I didn't mean what I said about wanting someone else to be my wife. I was just afraid I couldn't make you happy here in Royal. So I want you to know I'm willing to move, like Cord is doing."

Eyes dancing, she drew teasing circles along his back. "Thank you for that beautiful offer, and a couple of weeks ago, I might have been wrongheaded enough to have accepted. But now I know my heart and my future are here in Royal."

He couldn't believe his ears or his luck. More than luck, this was a Christmas miracle beyond any he could have imagined. And right on schedule as the night slid into Christmas Eve.

Jesse looked into the eyes of the woman he knew he would love for the rest of his life. "Merry Christmas, Esme. You're the best gift I could have ever received."

"And Merry Christmas to you, cowboy." She pulled his Stetson off and dropped it on her head. "I can promise you, the celebrating has only just begun."

Epilogue

Esme clutched Jesse's hand, eager to hear the announcement of the Houston chapter's president, the news to be revealed just before the stroke of midnight at the New Year's Eve soiree. She was doing her best to seem even-keeled and not at all on edge.

The ballroom was packed with members from both clubs, wall-to-wall Texas powerhouses mingling under crystal chandeliers. The men were decked out in tuxedos and their best Stetsons. Designer gowns and jewels to rival royalty draped the women.

But no one outshone the man at her side. She stole a look up at Jesse, her heart in her throat.

They'd had a blissful Christmas week together before driving to Houston yesterday for this evening's New Year's Eve gala.

Esme had gotten dressed twice tonight. The first time, Jesse had peeled off her gown and messed her updo. But she didn't mind. Not one bit. She and Jesse had thrown their clothes on quickly, barely making it to the gala on time. Trying to restore order to her hair in the car ride over, she'd given up and brushed it into a sleek, straight fall down her back. She'd smoothed the wrinkles out of her maroon gown with her hands, the silver embellishments glistening in the dash lights.

No one seemed to notice her hastily-put-together look. She slid a smoky-eyed glance up at Jesse. His knowing smile promised a repeat of earlier. An answering heat rose in her.

Her father and Ryder both appeared to be a bundle of nerves, even though they were making nice with each other, Angela smiling between them.

Her sister seemed happy. Genuinely happy. A sight that had been missing for what felt like ages.

And Jesse stepped right up like he'd known them forever. She appreciated how supportive he was of her family as a whole, and hoped to help him grow closer to his sister, Janet.

The music shifted from a fast dance number to a softer tune as the chairwoman for the nomination committee walked around the champagne fountain.

Abigail Langley Price, a stunning redhead in a bold sequined gown, had been instrumental in allowing women to join the Texas Cattleman's Club.

Abigail climbed the steps to take the microphone. "Well, I imagine everyone is eager to hear the election results." She paused playfully before continuing, "And I won't keep you in suspense a second longer. I'll start with the board members."

She pulled out a card and slid on cat's-eye reading glasses. She read name after name off the list with a flourish, waiting for the applause to wane after each announcement. And every time neither Ryder nor her father was called, nerves ratcheted higher in Esme's stomach with the growing possibility the president would be one of them.

The woman smiled out at the audience. "There are only two more board positions to fill before I announce the first president of the Texas Cattleman's Club, Houston branch. Are you ready?"

The crowd roared in response. Esme's gaze skittered over to her father. She mouthed "good luck" from across the room. Sterling winked at her, inclining his head before turning his attention back to the stage.

Jesse squeezed her hand, a gesture of warmth and support that flooded her. Made her feel invincible. Like anything and everything was possible.

"There's a bit of a twist. We have a tie for the last two board positions, both having gained equal

support. Our last two positions will be filled by...
Sterling Perry and Ryder Currin."

Neither man had won the bid for president?

Shock tingled through Esme, a sentiment she
suspected she wasn't alone in feeling. Whispers
zipped from person to person. If not Sterling or
Ryder, then who?

The woman tapped the microphone to regain
control of the room. "It is now my honor, as one of
the first women to be admitted to the Royal chapter
of the Texas Cattleman's Club, to announce your
president..." A drumroll rippled from the band, then
stopped. "Elected with an overwhelming amount
of write-in votes...Angela Perry."

Angela?

Without a second's hesitation, the crowd erupted
into deafening applause and shouts of approval. And
as Esme thought about it, she couldn't imagine anyone better for the job than her sister. She hoped
her father and Ryder would be supportive, as well.
Angling to look, she found both men holding their
hands high in applause as Angela made her way
to the stage.

Her sister was a vision in an off-the-shoulder
gown of gold tulle with the tiniest shimmer. "Thank
you, everyone, for the vote of confidence." Angela
pressed a hand to her chest, breathless with surprise.
"I'm stunned, to say the least. But honored and excited to lead the Houston chapter as we launch."

She waited for the applause to die down. "I'm especially pleased to serve with my father and my fiancé on the board."

More applause and cheers rippled through the partiers. Jesse let out a whoop. Esme's heart nearly burst as her smile grew even wider.

"I hope you'll indulge me a moment longer as my fiancé and I share some news of our own." Angela held out a hand to Ryder, her engagement ring glinting. She waved for him to join her on stage. He climbed the steps, his face beaming with pride.

Angela looked up at him, their love for each other clear for all to see. "We were given the best Christmas present of all. We're expecting our first child together."

The cheers and applause doubled in a rousing endorsement followed by glasses lifted in toast. Partiers converged around the couple and Esme knew she didn't stand a chance of getting to her sister anytime soon. But that was okay. They had months to celebrate.

Plans were already flowering in her mind for a joint baby shower for both of her sisters. Twins celebrating the births of their first children. Esme was truly happy for them.

Just as she knew they would be happy for her when her day came.

She looked up at Jesse, wondering aloud, "Are

you feeling the baby urge? I know you want children. And so do I."

Jesse kissed the inside of her wrist before drawing her hand to rest against his heart. Stars and promises glimmered in those green eyes.

"Someday. But first, I want us to have time together, to get to know each other, to build a foundation for our future." He kissed the tip of her nose. "But at the risk of sounding too practical, I want us to have time to savor falling more and more in love with each other."

"That's beautiful. Underneath all that rancher practicality, you really do have a sentimental heart, full of emotions as messy as your desk."

"My desk?" He cocked his head to the side, a laugh spluttering out.

"No need to look offended. I think all that clutter is endearing." She remembered the time they'd gotten hot and heavy there, a place that had helped her see who Jesse Stevens really was inside.

"Well, then, I'm more than happy to have a messy office."

The countdown to midnight started, the partiers chiming in until the forty-five-second mark was a thunderous echo of numbers. He pulled her close, swaying with her to the music, then spinning her out onto the balcony.

"How smart of you to have come out here ahead of the crowd to see the fireworks."

"Actually, I brought you out here to tell you how much I love you."

She smiled, her heart full of happiness like a champagne glass full of bubbles. "You've already told me."

"It's something I look forward to telling you every day." He held her tighter. Closer. Their bodies melting into one. Into a promise of forever.

"Now, isn't that convenient? Because I love you, too, and I enjoy telling you again and again." She teased her fingers along the hair at the base of his neck. "I can't believe how lucky we are."

"What a way to ring in the new year."

"And how wonderfully perfect we'll get to share the midnight kiss."

His low growl of approval rumbled between them as he angled down to take her up on that kiss.

A kiss that set her senses on fire. Their love made everything all the more special.

And as she arched up on her toes to press herself even closer, she could have sworn the fireworks had already started.

* * * * *

#2701 DUTY OR DESIRE

The Westmoreland Legacy • by Brenda Jackson

Becoming guardian of his young niece is tough for Westmoreland neighbor Pete Higgins. But Myra Hollister, the irresistible new nanny with a dangerous past, pushes him to the brink. Will desire for the nanny distract him from duty to his niece?

#2702 TEMPTING THE TEXAN

Texas Cattleman's Club: Inheritance • by Maureen Child

When a family tragedy calls rancher Kellan Blackwood home to Royal, Texas, he's reunited with the woman he left behind, Irina Romanov. Can the secrets that drove them apart in the first place bring them back together?

#2703 THE RIVAL

Dynasties: Mesa Falls • by Joanne Rock

Media mogul Devon Salazar is suspicious of the seductive new tour guide at Mesa Falls Ranch. Sure enough, Regina Flores wants to take him down after his father destroyed her family. But attraction to her target might take her down first...

#2704 RED CARPET REDEMPTION

The Stewart Heirs • by Yahrah St. John

Dane Stewart is a Hollywood heartthrob with a devilish reputation. When a sperm bank mishap reveals he has a secret child with the beautiful but guarded Iris Turner, their intense chemistry surprises them both. Can this made-for-the-movies romance last?

#2705 ONE NIGHT TO RISK IT ALL

One Night • by Katherine Garbera

After a night of passion, Inigo Velasquez learns that socialite Marielle Bisset is the woman who ruined his sister's marriage. A staged seduction to avenge his sister might quell his moral outrage... But will it quench his desire for Marielle?

#2706 TWIN SCANDALS

The Pearl House • by Fiona Brand

Seeking payback against the man who dumped her, Sophie Messena switches places with her twin on a business trip with billionaire Ben Sabin. When they are stranded by a storm, their attraction surges. But will past scandals threaten their chance at a future?

Get 4 FREE REWARDS!

We'll send you 2 FREE Books plus 2 FREE Mystery Gifts.

Harlequin® Desire books feature heroes who have it all: wealth, status, incredible good looks... everything but the right woman.

FREE
Value Over
$20

YES! Please send me 2 FREE Harlequin® Desire novels and my 2 FREE gifts (gifts are worth about $10 retail). After receiving them, if I don't wish to receive any more books, I can return the shipping statement marked "cancel." If I don't cancel, I will receive 6 brand-new novels every month and be billed just $4.55 per book in the U.S. or $5.24 per book in Canada. That's a savings of at least 13% off the cover price! It's quite a bargain! Shipping and handling is just 50¢ per book in the U.S. and $1.25 per book in Canada.* I understand that accepting the 2 free books and gifts places me under no obligation to buy anything. I can always return a shipment and cancel at any time. The free books and gifts are mine to keep no matter what I decide.

225/326 HDN GNND

Name (please print)

Address   Apt. #

City   State/Province   Zip/Postal Code

Mail to the **Reader Service:**
IN U.S.A.: P.O. Box 1341, Buffalo, NY 14240-8531
IN CANADA: P.O. Box 603, Fort Erie, Ontario L2A 5X3

Want to try 2 free books from another series? Call 1-800-873-8635 or visit www.ReaderService.com.

---

*Terms and prices subject to change without notice. Prices do not include sales taxes, which will be charged (if applicable) based on your state or country of residence. Canadian residents will be charged applicable taxes. Offer not valid in Quebec. This offer is limited to one order per household. Books received may not be as shown. Not valid for current subscribers to Harlequin Desire books. All orders subject to approval. Credit or debit balances in a customer's account(s) may be offset by any other outstanding balance owed by or to the customer. Please allow 4 to 6 weeks for delivery. Offer available while quantities last.

Your Privacy—The Reader Service is committed to protecting your privacy. Our Privacy Policy is available online at www.ReaderService.com or upon request from the Reader Service. We make a portion of our mailing list available to reputable third parties that offer products we believe may interest you. If you prefer that we not exchange your name with third parties, or if you wish to clarify or modify your communication preferences, please visit us at www.ReaderService.com/consumerschoice or write to us at Reader Service Preference Service, P.O. Box 9062, Buffalo, NY 14240-9062. Include your complete name and address.

HD20

A flash of pink moving around in his house made Kaegan frown when he recalled just who'd worn that particular color tonight. He glanced back at Sasha. "Tell Farley that I hope he starts feeling better. Good night." Without waiting for Sasha's response, he quickly walked off, heading inside his home.

He heard a noise coming from the kitchen. Moving quickly, he walked in to find Bryce Witherspoon on a ladder putting something in one of the cabinets. Anger, to a degree he hadn't felt in a long time, consumed him. Standing there in his kitchen on that ladder was the one and only woman he'd ever loved. The one woman he would risk his life for, and he recalled doing so once. She was the only woman who'd had his heart from the time they were in grade school. The only one he'd ever wanted to marry, have his babies. The only one who…

He realized he'd been standing there recalling things he preferred not remembering. What he should be remembering was that she was the woman who'd broken his heart. "What the hell are you doing in here, Bryce?"

His loud, booming voice startled her. She jerked around, lost her balance and came tumbling off the ladder. He rushed over and caught her in his arms before she could hit the floor. His chest tightened and his nerves, and a few other parts of his anatomy, kicked in the moment his hands and arms touched the body he used to know as well as his own. A body he'd introduced to passion. A body he'd—

"Put me down, Kaegan Chambray!"

He started to drop her, just for the hell of it. She was such a damn ingrate. "Next time I'll just let you fall on your ass," he snapped, placing her on her feet and trying not to notice how beautiful she was. Her eyes were a cross of hazel and moss green, and were adorned by long eyelashes. She had high cheekbones and shoulder-length curly brown hair. Her skin was a gorgeous honey brown and her lips, although at the moment curved in a frown, had always been one of her most noticeable traits.

"Let go of my hand, Kaegan!"

Her sharp tone made him realize he'd been standing there staring at her. He fought to regain his senses. "What are you doing, going through my cabinets?"

She rounded on him, tossing all that beautiful hair out of her face. "I was on that ladder putting your spices back in the cabinets."

He crossed his arms over his chest. "Why?"

"Because I was helping you tidy up after the party by putting things away."

She had to be kidding. "I don't need your help."

"Fine! I'll leave, then. You can take Vashti home."

Take Vashti home? What the hell was she talking about? He was about to ask when Vashti burst into the kitchen. "What in the world is going on? I heard the two of you yelling and screaming all the way in the bathroom."

Kaegan turned to Vashti. "What is she talking about, me taking you home? Where's Sawyer?"

"He got a call and had to leave. I asked Bryce to drop me off at home. I also asked her to assist me in helping you straighten up before we left."

"I don't need help."

Bryce rounded on him. "Why don't you tell her what you told me? Namely, that you don't need *my* help."

He had no problem doing that. Glancing back at Vashti, he said. "I don't need Bryce's help. Nor do I want it."

Bryce looked at Vashti. "I'm leaving. You either come with me now or he can take you home."

Vashti looked from one to the other and then threw up her hands in frustration. "I'm leaving with you, Bryce. I'll be out to the car in a minute."

When Bryce walked out of the kitchen, Kaegan turned to Vashti. "You had no right asking her to stay here after the party to do anything, Vashti. I don't want her here. The only reason I even invited her is because of you."

Kaegan had seen fire in Vashti's eyes before, but it had never been directed at him. Now it was. She crossed the room and he had a mind to take a step back, but he didn't. "I'm sick and tired of you acting like an ass where Bryce is concerned, Kaegan. When will you wake up and realize what you accused her of all those years ago is not true?"

He glared at her. "Oh? Is that what she told you? News flash—you weren't there, Vashti, and I know what I saw."

"Do you?"

"Yes. So, you can believe the lie she's telling you all you want, but I know what I saw that night."

Vashti drew in a deep breath. "Do you? Or do you only know what you think you saw?"

Then without saying anything else, she turned and walked out of the kitchen.

SPECIAL EXCERPT FROM

HARLEQUIN®
Desire

*Becoming guardian of his young niece is tough
for Westmoreland neighbor Pete Higgins.
But Myra Hollister, the irresistible new nanny with a
dangerous past, pushes him to the brink. Will desire for
the nanny distract him from duty to his niece?*

Read on for a sneak peek at
Duty or Desire
by New York Times *bestselling author Brenda Jackson!*

"That's it, Peterson Higgins, no more. You've had three servings already," Myra said, laughing, as she guarded the pan of peach cobbler on the counter.

He stood in front of her, grinning from ear to ear. "You should not have baked it so well. It was delicious."

"Thanks, but flattery won't get you any more peach cobbler tonight. You've had your limit."

He crossed his arms over his chest. "I could have you arrested, you know."

Crossing her arms over her own chest, she tilted her chin and couldn't stop grinning. "On what charge?"

The charge that immediately came to Pete's mind was that she was so darn beautiful. Irresistible. But he figured that was something he could not say.

She snapped her fingers in front of his face to reclaim his attention. "If you have to think that hard about a charge, then that means there isn't one."

"Oh, you'll be surprised what all I can do, Myra."

She tilted her head to the side as if to look at him better. "Do tell, Pete."

Her words—those three little words—made a full-blown attack on his senses. He drew in a shaky breath, then touched her chin. She blinked, as if startled by his touch. "How about 'do show,' Myra?"

Pete watched the way the lump formed in her throat and detected her shift in breathing. He could even hear the pounding of her heart. Damn, she smelled good, and she looked good, too. Always did.

"I'm not sure what 'do show' means," she said in a voice that was as shaky as his had been.

He tilted her chin up to gaze into her eyes, as well as to study the shape of her exquisite lips. "Then let me demonstrate, Ms. Hollister," he said, lowering his mouth to hers.

The moment he swept his tongue inside her mouth and tasted her, he was a goner. It took every ounce of strength he had to keep the kiss gentle when he wanted to devour her mouth with a hunger he felt all the way in his bones. A part of him wanted to take the kiss deeper, but then another part wanted to savor her taste. Honestly, either worked for him as long as she felt the passion between them.

He had wanted her from the moment he'd set eyes on her, but he'd fought the desire. He could no longer do that. He was a man known to forego his own needs and desires, but tonight he couldn't.

Whispering close to her ear, he said, "Peach cobbler isn't the only thing I could become addicted to, Myra."

Will their first kiss distract him from his duty?

Find out in
Duty or Desire
by New York Times *bestselling author Brenda Jackson.*

Available December 2019 wherever
Harlequin® Desire books and ebooks are sold.

Harlequin.com